Woman at the Well

By

Rev. C. J. Molmen

ISBN: 1-4033-1979-0 (e-book)
ISBN: 1-4033-1980-4 (Paperback)

This book is printed on acid free paper.

1stBooks – rev. 08/14/02

Acknowledgments

My wife, Hazel, didn't marry a preacher, but she adapted to being a preacher's wife; and was invaluable to me in my ministry. Neither did she marry a writer, but she adapted to being a writer's wife as well; and her patience and understanding during the long hours of neglect precipitated by the writing of this book made its completion possible. I want to acknowledge the interest and assistance my church, Bell Avenue Church, and the church administrator, John Robertson, provided in the preparation of my manuscript. Last, but certainly not least, I want to thank my Christian friends, too numerous to name individually, whose interest in my book was a constant source of encouragement.

Chapter One

Zanah, dancing and whirling around the room, gyrated and undulated to the beat of the tambourine she held - alternately banging it against her hip, and then with her two hands above her head. Before her, she saw in the flickering light from the oil lamps, the faces of five inebriated men, grinning like imps for the privilege of groping her body and touching her breasts. Dancing close to them, she taunted and teased them with her sexually provocative movements and, as they lunged for her, glided safely out of reach, laughing and mocking them. Clods! Boors! She despised them all, especially Mishtar with whom she lived. He it was who forced her to perform for his drunken friends - exposing her to their rude catcalls and lewd expressions - as if she was community property. Refusing to do his will resulted in a beating.

Zanah did, however, derive some satisfaction from arousing their libido, and then leaving them with their devious desires unfulfilled. And she felt good about herself, knowing she was attractive and possessed the physical attributes the men desired - although well aware she wasn't much finer than they were. She lacked the education, manners and polish that mark a lady and attract men of wealth, refinement and position - besides, there weren't any men like that in Sychar.

Mishtar, a Samaritan like Zanah, but twenty years older than her, dominated and abused her, requiring her to cater to his every whim and fancy. Mishtar's social life amounted to nothing more than nightly forays with friends to Spyros' inn, where it was he insisted Zanah dance for their pleasure. Although she enjoyed the attention, she felt demeaned because Mishtar not only wasn't offended by the men's demeanor, he actually encouraged them. She received no pay other than the wine the men bought for her - likely the reason Mishtar insisted on her dancing. He didn't have to pay for her wine. After a night of drinking, Mishtar was particularly demanding and abusive - often sexually assaulting her repeatedly. Zanah never deluded herself into thinking Mishtar loved her.

Spyros' inn wasn't much of an inn, but then Sychar wasn't much of a village. Situated on the south slope of Mount Ebal, Sychar consisted of fewer than twenty single story, flat-roofed limestone houses - most having but one room - and an equal number of leanto's and small stables for sheep, goats and donkeys. Other than Spyros' inn, there were no businesses in Sychar. Spyros and his wife, Iona, who were Greek, owned and operated the inn. Spyros, a short, thin, wiry man looked older than his fifty years - likely the result of running an inn in a place like Sychar. Iona, at five feet-five, and nearly as tall as Spyros, was almost as round as she was tall. Younger than Spyros by a couple of years, Iona looked much younger and was far more jovial. Noone ever knew, or bothered to ask, how or why Spyros came to own an inn in a place like Sychar.

The inn, similar to the other limestone buildings, except larger, consisted of living quarters for Spyros and Iona, a kitchen, dining room that was used more for drinking than dining, and two small sleeping rooms - seldom occupied, there being few guests. The dining room was the site for Zanah's dancing - as ordered by

Mishtar. Tables and benches were shoved aside to make room.

It was well past the second watch when Spyros, telling the men to go home, began snuffing out the oil lamps. Having consumed too much wine - Mishtar more than Zanah - they leaned on one another for support. Weaving their way along the rock-strewn path leading to Mishtar's house, he cursed every rock he stumbled over. Falling several times, he blamed Zanah for letting him fall. Noticing Mishtar's mood growing uglier, Zanah hoped he was too drunk to want any sexual favors tonight, for he always treated her roughly when he was drunk. She dreaded entering the house, but when Mishtar immediately unrolled his sleeping mat, placed it near the fireplace and fell into a drunken sleep, Zanah breathed a sigh of relief. Unrolling her own mat, she placed it alongside Mishtar and laid down.

****

The rays from the morning sun beat down on Mishtar, causing him to stir. Raising up on one elbow, he looked at Zanah still sleeping soundly. He sat upright, stretching and scratching, rubbing his eyes and licking his lips while swallowing repeatedly in an effort to work up some saliva and rid himself of the foul taste in his mouth. Getting up from the mat, he stumbled across the room to the washstand and water pot. He leaned on the washstand with one hand for support, while reaching for the water pot with the other. Tilting the pot to fill the basin, he saw it was empty. Looking into the reserve water jar, he saw it too was empty. Slamming the water pot down hard on top of the washstand, he was furious. Turning toward Zanah, who remained undisturbed by the commotion, he hollered out in anger.

"Woman! Get up and get some water!" Zanah gave no indication she heard him. In three giant strides, Mishtar bolted across the room and, hovering over Zanah, bellowed even louder. "Woman, I said get up and get some water!" Zanah mumbling something incoherent, rolled over, turning her back to Mishtar. Becoming more irritated by the minute, he grabbed Zanah by her garment, jerking her up from the mat.

"Are you going to get some water, or do I have to beat you first?"

Still not completely aroused, Zanah tried shaking the cobwebs out of her brain and pulling herself together. "I'll go later."

"You'll go now!" Mishtar exclaimed, striking Zanah in the face with his open hand, sending her reeling across the room. Rubbing her face, she said nothing. Her face smarted and throbbed with pain. It would leave a bruise, she knew. She hated Mishtar when he abused her like this. Crossing over to the washstand, she picked up the water pot. Mishtar had stomped out the door. Where he was going didn't concern her. He would be back. He always came back. She better get the water before he returned or there would be hell to pay.

The sun had started to take the chill out of the air. Unlike Zanah's mood, downcast and irritable, the morning was beautiful. Her face still stinging, she wondered what she could do about her situation - if anything. She knew Mishtar's temper always exploded whenever she crossed him or failed to obey his orders, and the end result was always the same - just as it was this time. But this altercation upset her more than the others. Must she go on living like this? Was there no way out? What if she just walked away? She wasn't married to him. There weren't any chains binding her. True, but how would she subsist? Find another man to take her in? He might prove to be worse than Mishtar - although she found that hard to believe. No, there wasn't any solution. Might as well put up with Mishtar and be done with it. At least it was better than sleeping on the ground and starving to death.

Zanah had ample time to think. It was nearly fifteen furlongs to the well - a good forty-five minute's walk. She recalled being told the patriarch, Jacob, dug this well hundreds of years ago. It was on the trade route that led from the port city, Caesarea, through the fertile valley between Mount Ebal and Mount Gerizim and on to Jerusalem. Caravans, traders and travelers stopped at the well to refresh themselves and water their camels and donkeys. Inhabitants from both villages, Sychar and Shechem, got their water from the well.

There would be others at the well, especially from Shechem, Zanah figured. Most folks went for water early in the day, before it got too hot. She despised the people from Shechem, especially Gabah, wife of Samuel, the Shechem Prefect. The Roman Procurator, Pontius Pilate, appointed Samuel to the office to help maintain law and order so Pilate could spend more time at his palace in Caesarea - not having to be involved in such trivial matters as street fights and domestic squabbles. The office was honorary more than authoritative but, according to Zanah, Gabah acted as if her husband was king and she was queen. Gabah thought she was superior to everyone else, and decidedly better than anyone from Sychar. On second thought, Zanah concluded, didn't everyone from Shechem feel that way about folks from Sychar? Shechem was like fine wine, and Sychar was the dregs in the bottom of the vat.

Arriving at the well, Zanah saw, just as she had expected, Gabah and her crowd of women were there. She knew there was no way of ignoring or avoiding Gabah - Gabah would make sure of. that.

"Well, well," Gabah crowed. "If it isn't the whore of Sychar. What happened to your face, dearie? Run into a door?" Gabah roared with laughter while the other women, hiding behind Gabah's skirts, tittered.

Gabah was her usual insulting self. She was the leader. The women with her merely gave her moral support - why, Zanah could never understand. What they saw in Gabah baffled her. Ignoring Gabah, Zanah tried approaching the well, but Gabah crowded in front of her and pushed her aside. In no mood for an altercation - she had already had one with Mishtar, and one was too many - Zanah allowed Gabah to have her fun. After several minutes, Gabah permitted Zanah to draw her water, continuing to insult her as she did.

"Who are you sleeping with tonight?" Gabah asked as Zanah prepared to leave. "Maybe he'll bruise your other cheek." Seething with anger, Zanah failed to notice Gabah stick her foot out to trip her. Zanah fell to the ground, dropping her water pot, breaking it to pieces, soaking her to the skin and muddying her clothes. Picking herself up and brushing herself off as best she could, she saw the women doubled over with laughter. She saw Gabah's fat, round face framed as if it was floating in a sea of red. With clenched fist, she took aim at the face, and caught Gabah squarely on her jaw, knocking her down. The laughter stopped. Without waiting for any further repercussions, Zanah hurried home. This has turned out to be a really ugly day, she concluded.

Arriving home, Zanah saw Mishtar was back. She wondered what kind of mood he was in. When she would tell him what happened, she expected he would be angry - especially since she was returning without any water. Judging from his mood when he left, she figured he would all but kill her. Steeling herself for the confrontation, she cautiously opened the door. "Where's the water?" Mishtar's voice was calm. His anger had subsided. Zanah heaved a sigh of relief.

"I broke the jar."

"Broke it! How?"

Relating the skirmish at the well, Zanah waited for Mishtar's reaction. She hoped it wouldn't rekindle his anger. One more upheaval would be more than she could handle. "You sure know how to pick 'em."

Mishtar shook his head hopelessly. "Of all people, why Gabah?" At least he wasn't angry, Zanah noted.

"She didn't leave me any choice."

"Well, you can bet you haven't heard the last of it."

"Why? What can she do about it now?"

"It's not what she can do, but what her husband can do."

"He doesn't have any authority."

"No, but Gabah thinks he does. She won't let him rest until he does something - and he does have some influence."

****

About the ninth hour, Zanah and Mishtar heard a loud pounding on the door. Opening the door, Mishtar was confronted by two Roman soldiers.

"Woman named Zanah live here?" One soldier inquired in a brusque manner.

"What do you want with her?" Mishtar asked.

"Is she here?" The soldier asked, ignoring Mishtar's question.

"I'm Zanah," she said, stepping out from behind Mishtar.

"You will come with us."

"Why? What have I done?" It was a senseless question. Gabah was already seeking her revenge.

"Our orders are to deliver you to the Shechem Prefect; that's all we know. You will come with us."

Taking Zanah's arm, the soldier ushered her out the door. One soldier leading the way, the other soldier bringing up the rear and Zanah in between, the trio marched down the path toward Shechem. As they walked, neither soldier spoke. Zanah pondered this most recent development. She was more than a little put out with Mishtar. He didn't say anything on her behalf. She didn't expect him to confront the soldiers, but he could have taken more of a stand than he did. At the very least, he could have offered to go along and give her moral support - that is if he cared anything at all about her. Further evidence, she concluded, he didn't.

Turning her thoughts toward meeting the Prefect, she wondered what he was like - having never met him. Except for going to the market on occasion to buy produce, she didn't have much to do with Shechem. Was the Prefect anything like Gabah? God help her if he was. What did Gabah tell him? It must've been a good story to make Samuel send two soldiers for her. "I'll bet she didn't tell him what she did," Zanah said to herself. "Well, I' II set the record straight."

Entering the building housing the Prefect's office, Zanah stood before Samuel, one soldier on each side of her. She couldn't believe her eyes. Samuel was nothing like Gabah, at least not in appearance. Gabah was big any way one looked at her - tall, fat, heavy. Samuel was a little man, not more than five foot six or seven, weighing no more than a hundred forty pounds, Zanah guessed. No wonder Gabah was so domineering. Samuel was probably afraid to cross her. Gabah would squash him like a bug. The thought made her chuckle to herself.

"You are accused of assault and battery and public brawling." The Prefect's voice snapped Zanah out of her musing. "How do you plead?" Nothing in Samuel's voice indicated he was weak or timid.

"Sir, I can explain…"

"I'm not interested in explanations. Did you, or did you not assault Gabah?"

"Yes, Sir, but…"

"That's all. I fine you fifty pence."

"Sir, I don't have any money."

"Then I order you confined to the guardhouse for three days."

"Please, Sir…"

"Take her away," Samuel commanded with a wave of his hand. The soldiers, taking Zanah by her arms, escorted her out of the office.

The guardhouse was a small room in the same barracks where the soldiers were quartered. Entrance was gained through an outside door - there being no inside door connecting the guardhouse with the rest of the barracks. Zanah saw that the room was bare except for a chair and a mat to sleep on. A small window with bars on it let in light and afforded her a view of at least part of the outside world. It wasn't as bad as some prisons she had heard about - or some she had been in for that matter. There weren't any rats, and it was reasonably clean. Sitting on the mat and leaning her back against the wall, Zanah turned her thoughts back to Samuel. He wasn't as meek and mild as he looked. Knowing Gabah wasn't one to allow anyone to dominate her, Zanah wondered how she and Samuel got along. They couldn't both be boss. After mulling it over, Zanah thought she had the answer. Gabah so dominated Samuel in their private life that, when he was in his office, he took advantage of his position to be the domineering one. That had to be the answer, Zanah concluded.

Having figured Samuel out, at least to her own satisfaction, Zanah turned her thoughts to Mishtar. She had plenty of time to think - three days in fact. Time was the only thing she did have. Would Mishtar come to see her? She doubted it. Samuel probably wouldn't permit it anyway. When her time was up, she guessed she would go back to Mishtar - if he would take her back. What other alternative was there? What if Mishtar wouldn't take her back - what then? The possibility disturbed her.

Zanah heard someone unbolting the door. A soldier entered, bringing her supper. She had been so occupied with her thoughts she hadn't noticed the sun had receded behind the mountains, and it was getting dark. Setting the dish on the chair, the soldier looked down on Zanah, who remained seated on the mat. "Brought your supper." Zanah noticed what she took to be a depraved look in his eyes. She felt uncomfortable, and offered no reply. Seating himself on the mat alongside her, he spoke in a smooth, solicitous manner and put his arm around her. "Be nice to me and I can make things easier for you; maybe get your sentence reduced." He tried drawing her close.

Shoving his arm away, Zanah jumped to her feet and took her stance against the wall on the opposite side of the room. He was not to be so easily rebuffed. Scrambling to his feet, and placing his body in front of her, he pinned her against the wall with his arms.

"Ya got fire," he sneered. "I like my women to have fire."

He attempted to kiss her.

"I' m not your woman!" Zanah brought her knee up hard on the soldier's private parts, causing him to double over in pain. Still bent over, he moved toward the door. Looking back at Zanah, he scowled, "You had your chance. I can make it rough on you too." He left. Zanah slid down the wall and sat on the floor, relieved he was gone.

The following morning Zanah was awakened by someone unbolting the door. Her heart pounded, and she jumped to her feet. Was it that soldier again? Seeing it was a different soldier, she felt a little easier - although she had no reason to believe he would be any less solicitous.

"Breakfast," he said, setting the dish on the chair. "What did you do to Antonio?" Zanah noticed a sly look of amusement on his face.

"Antonio?"

"Yes, the soldier who brought your supper last night?"

"Oh, him! He tried to kiss me, and I kneed him where it would hurt the most."

"I figured it was something like that," he chuckled. His manner and voice told Zanah she had nothing to fear from him.

"He's like that. Thinks he's quite the lover, but don't worry about him. No doubt he got what he deserved." He left. Zanah heard the bolt on the door slide shut.

The next two days passed without incident. Antonio never brought her meals or stepped into her room again - for which she was grateful. The other soldiers were courteous enough. She imagined at one time or another they had encountered Gabah themselves, and reasoned that whatever Zanah did, Gabah like Antonio had it coming. Perhaps the soldiers even felt a little sympathy toward her. At any rate, they certainly acted differently than - what was his name - Antonio?

Zanah heard the bolt in the door slide and a soldier entered. "Come with me," he commanded. "The Prefect wants to see you."

Following the soldier into the Prefect's office, Zanah stood before Samuel. Certain she understood

Samuel's brusque manner better now, she even felt a touch of pity for the man. Poor man; he had to live with Gabah.

"You have served your sentence," Samuel said. "I hope you have learned your lesson."

"Yes, Sir."

"If you ever come before me again, I will be very hard on you. You are free to go." Samuel dismissed her with a wave of his hand.

Thanking him, Zanah left the office and came face to face with Antonio. He glared at her. Glaring back, she stepped around him and continued on her way. Antonio made no effort to stop her.

On her way back to Sychar, Zanah reflected on some things - like her three days in the guardhouse. It wasn't too bad. Small price to pay for the privilege of punching Gabah, and it was probably sufficient punishment to get Gabah off Samuel's back. Zanah recalled days with Mishtar that were much worse - plenty of them. Except for the incident with Antonio, Zanah couldn't really complain about her incarceration. Who did Antonio think he was anyway?

Rev. C. J. Molmen

Not that she was so virtuous, she admitted to herself, but she did have some scruples. She was loyal to Mishtar.

Had Mishtar been as loyal to her these past three days? It depended on whether or not he felt the need for sexual gratification during that time. Mishtar didn't know the meaning of the word, "Loyalty." The possibility he might have found someone else troubled Zanah. There being no other option, she planned to take up with Mishtar right where she left off. But what if he had other plans?

Standing at the door to the house, Zanah hesitated a moment before entering - not knowing what kind of reception awaited her. Cautiously shoving the door open, she saw Mishtar was napping, or sleeping off a drunk - she couldn't tell which. The sound of the door opening aroused him. He was alone. Zanah hadn't considered what she would do if he was in a foul mood, or had another woman with him. Probably end up in the guardhouse again, she reckoned.

"You back?" Mishtar asked, as if her presence wasn't sufficient evidence.

"I'm back."

"Planning on staying?"

"If you want me."

"Suit yourself." Mishtar turned his back to Zanah, and went over to the washstand. Pouring some water in the basin, he splashed water on his face. Zanah wondered who got the water for him. He wasn't about to fetch it himself.

"There's one thing I ask." Zanah didn't wait for Mishtar to ask what that one thing was. "I don' t want to go to the well mornings. I don't want to get into it with Gabah. I'll go evenings."

Mishtar turned, water dripping from his beard. "You're not in a position to make any demands. Go whenever you like, but don' t run out of water like the last time."

****

Zanah, taking up the water jar, walked toward the well. The memory of the last time she had walked along this path was still fresh in her mind. She could almost feel Mishtar's blow, her throbbing face and the

21

misery she was in. Recalling the encounter with Gabah, she shuddered. She hoped this trip would be different - in a more pleasant way. Hopefully there wouldn't be anyone else at the well this time of day.

That hope made her feel light-hearted and put a spring in her step. Even little sparrows flitting from one scraggly bush to another as she passed caught her eye. The turtle doves defiantly refused to fly until nearly stepped on. Strange, she never noticed them before, or if she did, she didn't give any attention to them. She saw the wild flowers, nettles and thistles struggling to grow in the crevices of the rocks, and thought how much her life was like theirs. She had a certain comeliness. Most men, and some women, considered her attractive - although not as beautiful and delicate as the flowers. Wasn't she struggling to survive in her environment? Mishtar, the men who frequented the inn, Gabah and her own wantonness were the rocks in her life. She was trying to survive among them. Reaching the well, Zanah set about drawing water.

"Will you give me a drink?" A voice asked.

Startled, Zanah turned to see a slight-built, bearded man sitting on the low, stone wall a few paces from the well. She had been so absorbed with her thoughts she had failed to notice him. Immediately, she recognized he was a Jew; seldom seen in Samaria.

"You are a Jew and I am a Samaritan woman. How is it you ask me for a drink knowing you Jews do not associate with Samaritans - even considering us your enemy?"

"If you knew the gift of God and who it is that asks you for a drink, you would have asked him and he would have given you living water," the stranger said.

"Sir, you have nothing to draw with and the well is deep. Where can you get this living water?" Approaching the stranger, Zanah grew more bold. "Are you greater than our father Jacob who gave us this well, and drank from it himself, as did his sons and his flocks and herds?"

"Everyone who drinks this water will be thirsty again, but whoever drinks the water I give him will never thirst. Indeed, the water I give him will become in him a spring of water welling up to eternal life."

The man spoke like no man Zanah had ever heard before, and she was captivated by his words. "Sir, give me this water so that I won't get thirsty and have to keep coming here to draw water." A proposition she deemed exceptionally attractive.

"Go call your husband and come back."

"I have no husband."

"You are right when you say you have no husband. The fact is you have had five husbands, and the man you now have is not your husband. What you have just said is quite true."

Surprised and overwhelmed by the stranger's knowledge of her past, Zanah said, "Sir, I can see you are a prophet. Our fathers worshiped on this mountain, but you Jews claim that the place where we must worship is in Jerusalem."

"Believe me, woman, a time is coming when you will worship the Father neither on this mountain or in Jerusalem. You Samaritans worship what you do not know, we worship what we do know, for salvation is from the Jews. Yet a time is coming and has now come when the true worshipers will worship the Father in

24

spirit and truth, for they are the kind of worshipers the Father seeks. God is spirit, and His worshipers must worship in spirit and truth."

Zanah was astonished by what the stranger said. "I know that Messiah is coming, and when he comes, he will explain everything to us."

"I who speak to you am He."

Before Zanah could respond, their conversation was interrupted by several men approaching - also Jews, she noticed. They acted surprised to see the stranger talking to her. They stared at her as if to say, "What do you want?" Turning to the stranger, who Zanah surmised must be their leader, they appeared to be asking him, "Why are you talking to her?"

Leaving her water jar behind, and without waiting to see or hear anything further, Zanah ran toward Sychar, exclaiming to everyone she met along the way, "Come, see a man who told me everything I did. Could this be the Christ?"

Zanah ran directly to Spyros' inn where she knew Mishtar and the others would be. Bursting through the door, she exclaimed, "Come, see a man who told me everything I did. Could this be the Christ?"

Taken aback by the sudden intrusion, and then realizing it was only Zanah, the men returned to their wine and conversation. Zanah wasn't going to be ignored. Grabbing Mishtar's arm, she pulled him off the bench.

"I tell you, I have talked to the Messiah," Zanah insisted.

"An' I've talked to Queen Cleopatra. Let go my arm! You're drunk!"

"I'm not drunk! I'm telling the truth. This man knew everything I ever did."

"Everybody in Sychar knows everything you ever did," Mishtar scoffed.

"But this man's a stranger. I never saw him before. He's a Jew."

"A Jew!?" One of the men exclaimed, becoming interested. "Here in Samaria?"

"No Jew would be caught dead in Samaria," another enjoined.

"Well, he's here, I tell you; and he has some more Jews with Him."

"Zanah, you sure you're not making this up?" Mishtar asked, beginning to show some interest - as were the other men.

"I swear. He said I had five husbands, and you are not my husband. He told me about some water, if you drink it, you will never be thirsty again. He said you have to worship God in spirit and in truth. He said He was Christ. Come, see for yourself."

Acknowledging Zanah couldn't be making all this up, and she wasn't hallucinating, the men pushed back their benches and rushed to the door. Hurrying toward the well, they told everyone they met, "Zanah thinks she's seen the Messiah." The small group that left the inn grew into a band of twenty or more, including some women. Time was of the essence for it was getting dark. Arriving at the well, they saw the man Zanah described. He was, indeed, a Jew and several more Jews were with Him. The man and His companions had just finished eating. Seeing the crowd, the one Zanah had talked to arose and spoke to them.

27

"I am Jesus, Son of Man. I have come to call you to repentance, for the kingdom of God is at hand. What this woman has told you is true. You come to this well for water to drink, but whoever drinks this water will be thirsty again. Whoever drinks the water I give him will never thirst again." The people stood silent, momentarily stunned by Jesus' words. Noone dared speak, let alone challenge or question Jesus. It was as though a spell had been cast over them.

"The hour is late," Jesus continued. "Go to your homes and come back in the morning. I will tell you the truth, and the truth will make you free." Turning to the men with Him, they retreated a short distance from the crowd.

For a moment - although it seemed much longer to Zanah - noone moved. Slowly, one by one, they began drifting back to Sychar.

"What did He mean, the truth will make us free?" Mishtar growled. "We' re not slaves." Zanah ignored the remark. Reaching home, Mishtar unrolled his sleeping mat, placed it near the fire, and went to sleep without any further comment; without so much as saying goodnight. Zanah unrolled her mat and laid it next to Mishtar's. Unable to sleep, she watched the reflection of the fire on the ceiling; mystified by this strange happening. Sleep finally overtook her.

****

The crowd gathering at the well the next morning was larger than the day before - numbering perhaps fifty or sixty people. During the night and pre-dawn, word about Jesus and His friends had gotten around. Zanah saw the crowd included many from Shechem, but didn't see Gabah among them - for which she was grateful. Zanah noted further, everyone who saw Jesus the day before, like herself, returned to the well; that is, much to her dismay, everyone except Mishtar. Didn't he believe Jesus is the Christ, or didn't he want to believe? She really wasn't sure what to believe herself. The sound of Jesus voice drew her attention.

"You are the salt of the earth," Jesus said. "But if the salt loses its saltiness, how can it be made salty again? It is no longer good for anything except to be thrown out and trampled by men."

Zanah was confused. Salt? What is this about salt? Why is he talking about salt instead of the kingdom? What does it mean? Was there some sort of hidden meaning? She felt uncomfortable not knowing; as if it was something she wasn't privileged to know. She didn't like secrets. The way the others were looking at each other, she knew they too were perplexed.

"Do not think that I have come to abolish the law or the prophets," Jesus said. "I have not come to abolish them but to fulfill them. I tell you the truth, until heaven and earth disappear, not the smallest letter, not the least stroke of a pen, will by any means disappear from the law until everything is accomplished. Anyone who breaks one of the least of these commandments and teaches others to do the same will be called least in the kingdom of heaven."

Zanah hung onto every word. Jesus went on talking now about murder. He said whoever murders faces the judgment - something she had always been told. But then Jesus said even if you are angry with someone, you face the judgment. She had never heard that before. She thought about the many times she had been angry with Mishtar and Gabah. Would she have to answer to God for all those times? The very thought made her tremble. Jesus spoke about adultery. He said if you commit adultery in your heart, you are as guilty as if you actually committed the act. Was Jesus talking about her? She felt terribly uneasy. After all, He had told her earlier she had been married five times and Mishtar wasn't her husband. She was certainly guilty of adultery, not once, but several times, no mistaking that. In fact, she was even now living in adultery. Not liking what she was hearing, she wanted to turn away. She felt guilty and ashamed, but an inner force compelled her to stay.

Jesus continued teaching in Samaria for another day, and even though Zanah believed everything Jesus said was directed toward her - he knew too much about her - she went to the well the second day anyway. The crowd was even larger than the day before. She wondered if others were experiencing the same guilt feeling she was. If they were, why did they keep coming back? For that matter, why did she keep coming back? Unable to persuade Mishtar to come with her, she shared everything Jesus said with him; but he wasn't interested. He kept saying there was always somebody coming along claiming to be the Messiah. They had all come and gone, amounting to nothing, he had said. As far as Mishtar was concerned, Jesus was just another one of those fanatics - crazies. Mishtar claimed the real Messiah wouldn't look or act like Jesus.

"And look at the rag-tag men he has with him," Mishtar said. "The real Messiah wouldn't run with such as them." Zanah was at a loss to provide a suitable argument. She was never successful arguing with Mishtar. If she pressed him too hard, or if he thought he was losing the argument, he became angry and abusive. It was true, however, she had to agree Mishtar was right. Jesus wasn't a pretentious figure, and the men with him were crude and ignorant. Still there was an aura about Him she couldn't explain.

Bright daylight had surrendered to dusk and gray shadows by the time Zanah returned home. Mishtar wasn't home. More than likely he was at the inn, she concluded. That's where he usually was at this hour.

She didn't feel like going to the inn, but she didn't feel like staying home alone either. Jesus' words had convicted her of her immoral, tumultuous life, and left her despondent. She was restless and unsettled - as if something within her remained unfulfilled and demanded to be consummated. Unable to shake the feeling, she went to the inn.

They were all there, Mishtar and all his friends. Seating herself alongside Mishtar, he poured her a cup of wine. Zanah toyed with the cup, but didn't drink. One of the men, becoming bored, asked Zanah to dance for them - her dancing always livened things up. She declined, saying she wasn't in the mood. An hour later when she and Mishtar made their way home, her melancholy persisted, and they never so much as uttered one word to each other.

Unrolling his sleeping mat, Mishtar invited Zanah to join him. He wanted to make love. Zanah didn't. Rejecting his invitation, she waited for Mishtar's anger to erupt - his invitation being the equivalent of a command. To her surprise, he remained relatively calm for a change.

"What's the matter with you? You didn't touch your drink, you wouldn't dance, you haven't said two words all night; and now you don't want to make love."

Leaning against the wall, arms folded across her chest and head bowed, she said, "I don't know. It just doesn't seem right - drinking, dancing and making love. Jesus said …"

"Jesus said! Jesus said!" Mishtar jumped up from the mat. Zanah winced, expecting him to strike her. "That's all you talk about lately."

"I can't help it. That's how I feel," Zanah said, sliding down the wall and sitting on the floor.

"I'll be glad when this Jesus is gone!"

"He's already gone," Zanah said, without looking up at Mishtar.

"Where'd He go?"

"Said something about Galilee."

"Galilee? Aha!" Mishtar exclaimed, clapping his hands together in triumph. "That proves He's a fake. Nothing good comes out of Galilee. Galilee's as bad as Samaria - maybe worse."

34

"Maybe so, but that doesn't change anything. I feel dirty and ashamed of myself."

"How long's that gonna last?" He hovered over her menacingly. Zanah didn't respond. "C'mon, Zanah, forget Jesus." He seated himself alongside her and drew her close. "You'll feel better." She pulled away from him and remained sullen. "So, that's how it is!" He leaped to his feet. "I' ve got no use for you then! Get out!" He shoved the door open, and stood there waiting for her to leave.

"Where will I go?"

"Go to Jesus for all I care! Just go!"

Knowing it was useless to resist or plead any further, she got up and stepped out into the darkness. She heard Mishtar slam the door behind her. The night had already slipped into its cold nightshirt, and it didn't take long before the cold dampness penetrated her body. Shivering, she pulled her cloak tightly around her.

Seeing a light burning in Spyros' inn - although it was well past closing time - she was drawn to it like a moth to a flame. Would Spyros let her sleep their tonight? It was Iona who answered Zanah's knock.

"Zanah? What are you doing out this time of night?" Iona asked, inviting Zanah in.

Relating briefly what had happened, Zanah asked Iona, "May I stay here tonight? I can't pay you, but I don't have any place to go."

"You poor dear. Of course you may stay."

Zanah didn't know Iona very well. Spyros was always the one who served them and told them when to go home. Iona remained in the background. Zanah found her to be very warm, friendly and caring. She fixed Zanah a bowl of lentil soup she kept on the fire. Thanking her, Zanah wrapped her cold hands around the bowl and sipped the soup. She felt the hot soup flow through her body. Strange, Zanah mused, you could know someone for years, like she had known Iona, and yet not really know them. Zanah didn't see or hear Spyros, assuming he was already in bed. While she ate her soup, Iona busied herself about the kitchen. Iona didn't ask any questions - a courtesy Zanah appreciated - and neither did Zanah volunteer any information. She preferred not to talk about what happened. Besides, Iona had probably guessed anyway.

"Come dear, I'll show you where you'll sleep."

She followed Iona into a small room containing a bed, chair, washstand, water jar and basin - that was all. Zanah noticed the bed in particular; having never slept on one - always a mat. Pushing down on the bed with the palms of her hands, it proved to be harder than it looked - but still not as hard as sleeping on a mat. Iona left the room, and Zanah drifted off to sleep.

Chapter Two

What Zanah thought would be a one night stay at Spyros' inn, at Iona's insistence, turned out to be an extended sojourn. Two months had passed since Mishtar evicted her and she began living at the inn, helping Iona. Iona was gentle and kind - qualities Zanah was not accustomed to. She never questioned Zanah about her past or her life with Mishtar - two subjects Zanah preferred not to discuss. Neither did Iona say how long she intended to let Zanah remain at the inn - another subject Zanah didn't want to think about. She was happy with things the way they were, and neither Spyros nor Iona indicated they were anxious for her to leave. That was good, but there was a downside.

Helping Iona called for Zanah to make daily trips to the well and to the market in Shechem; and that meant frequent encounters with Gabah. Gabah was always her acid-tongued self whenever they met. She never let Zanah forget her sordid past, the three days in the guardhouse, or being evicted by the likes of Mishtar - all fodder for Gabah's caustic remarks. Gabah, however, never resorted to physical abuse like she did that one day at the well. Much to Zanah's surprise, Gabah's needling didn't anger her as before - a development Zanah was unable to explain. Encounters with Mishtar, which occurred almost daily, were not as easily brooked.

Mishtar was unable to reconcile himself to life without Zanah. Not being in the habit of doing household chores, he didn't take to them readily or cheerfully - preferring instead to ignore them. Neither was he able to clear his conscience concerning the argument with Zanah. He knew he acted in haste and without provocation; yet he continued to fault Zanah. After all, he had allowed his temper to get the best of him and taken out his frustrations on Zanah before, and she always came crawling back. Their life together went on as before. Not this time - for which he blamed Iona. He didn't count on Zanah finding solace in Iona and refuge at the inn. If Iona had minded her own business, Zanah would already be back with him.

Evicting Zanah, or fixing the blame on Iona, didn't put an end to Mishtar's nightly forays to the inn. Although Zanah no longer danced for the men, or for her own satisfaction, she did help Spyros serve their wine and replenish their cups. Whenever she was within reach, Mishtar grabbed her and made rude advances - which Zanah forcefully resisted. When she was beyond his reach, he made lewd, suggestive remarks - which Zanah managed to ignore. Mishtar dared not be more aggressive at the inn for fear Spyros would eject him and forbid him from patronizing the inn. If Mishtar couldn't adjust to life without Zanah, he would never be able to adjust to life apart from the inn. Nevertheless, his presence and vulgar overtures made Zanah uncomfortable. Away from the inn, Mishtar's conduct was even more reprehensible. Knowing Zanah made daily trips to the well and market, whenever he felt the need, Mishtar laid in ambush and forced himself upon her. He was much stronger than she, and she believed it was more expedient to give in than to resist. If she resisted, she knew Mishtar would tear her clothing, beat her and take what he wanted anyway.

Then Iona would ask questions. Zanah didn't want to burden Iona with her problems. As long as she remained in Sychar, or anywhere near Mishtar, Zanah knew these incidents would continue. The assaults were humiliating and degrading, leaving her feeling cheap and dirty. She had laid with Mishtar more times than she could count without feeling defiled. Why did she feel that way now? Was it the idea of being raped rather than being a willing participant? Whatever it was, Mishtar left her no choice. She would have to leave Sychar or endure Mishtar.

****

Spyros and Iona were pleasantly surprised with the arrival of long-time friend, Leukas Agnos and his slave, Nicholas. Leukas, a Greek like Spyros and Iona, had been a friend of theirs when they lived in Greece. He was a trader, currently out of Alexandria, and had delivered a consignment of Egyptian linen to a merchant in Jerusalem, and reinvested in some finished garments which he proposed selling in Capernaum. Since one of the trade routes to Capernaum passed through the valley between Shechem and Sychar, Leukas decided to visit his old friends.

While Leukas, Spyros and Iona exchanged pleasantries, Zanah's eyes fell approvingly on Nicholas, also a Greek. She noted he didn't participate in the conversation, but stood tall and erect, like a soldier, behind Leukas; ready to enact whatever orders Leukas might convey. This in itself was not unusual conduct for a slave, as Zanah was well aware, but she perceived he didn't look or act the part of a typical slave. For one thing, his manner and appearance gave him an air of dignity and refinement not found in most slaves. If they had dignity before being enslaved, they usually lost it. Not so, Nicholas. He wore his light brown hair closely and neatly trimmed, and he was clean shaven. Lively blue eyes made his countenance bright and alert, not stoic or sullen like so many slaves. What a beautiful specimen of manhood - so unlike the crude, boorish Mishtar and the other men she knew.

For another thing, Leukas didn't belittle or disparage Nicholas as one might a slave, but spoke to him respectfully, as one might his peers. This strange association caused Zanah to wonder how Nicholas became a slave. She noted, however, Nicholas was careful to maintain his station and not take advantage of Leukas' attitude toward him. Upon orders from Leukas, Nicholas excused himself and went to the stable to relieve the donkeys of their burden, feed them and bed them down.

Spyros, Iona and Leukas sat down to supper, Zanah serving them. The three continued relating events that had occurred since they last saw each other. Zanah couldn't put Nicholas out of her mind; nor did she try. We have something in common, she deduced. Although she wasn't a slave, her position was similar to Nicholas'. She didn't fit in with Spyros, Iona and Leukas either, and she wasn't invited to participate in the conversation. Like Nicholas, she stood off to the side awaiting orders from Iona. There wasn't much difference, she concluded. Nicholas did not return. She presumed he would remain in the stable with the donkeys and merchandise for the night.

Supper finished and the conversation lagging, Iona suggested Leukas must be tired after his journey, and offered to show him to his room. Zanah cleared the table and set the kitchen in order. She overheard Iona question Leukas concerning Nicholas' well-being, to which Leukas assured her Nicholas would be fine. Putting some lentil soup in a bowl and gathering up a blanket, Zanah took them to the stable. She saw Nicholas was already bedded down on a pile of straw with a coarse camel's hair robe covering him. Upon Zanah's arrival, he sat up.

"Brought you some soup and a blanket," Zanah said, handing him the bowl of soup, and setting the blanket down beside him. "Thank, you," Nicholas said, taking the bowl from her. "How is it you speak to me and serve me, a slave?"

Stunned and embarrassed, Zanah realized how brazen and unconventional her actions were. Regaining her composure, she said, "I don't know. Maybe it's because a Jew named Jesus spoke to me, a woman and a Samaritan."

"Do you know this Jesus?" Nicholas asked, believing it was acceptable to continue the conversation. Eyeing Zanah, he lifted the bowl to his lips. He saw warmth and friendliness in her soft, brown eyes.

"No. I met Him one time at Jacob's well." Sitting down on the pile of straw near Nicholas, Zanah continued. "He asked me to give Him a drink, and then He told me all about myself." She picked up a straw and put one end in her mouth. "Do you know Him?"

"No, but we have just come from Jerusalem, and there's much talk about him there," Nicholas said, sipping the soup. "Very good soup."

"Thank, you. What do they say about Him?"

"Well, it depends on who you talk to. The religious leaders hate Him."

"Why?"

"They accuse Him of blasphemy. He claims to be the Messiah."

"Yes, that's what He told me. But why should they hate Him for that?"

"I'm not sure. Something about being afraid He will cause trouble with the Romans, and jeopardize their freedom." He raised the bowl to his lips.

"How awful. What do the others say?"

"The Romans hate Him too, especially the government. The legionnaires have orders to arrest anyone who is a follower of His."

"I don't understand," Zanah said, shaking her head. "He seemed so humble and gentle - harmless."

"That may be true, but He says He is a king and keeps talking about His kingdom. That doesn't set well with Pilate."

"I suppose not. What do the people say?"

"They're afraid to say anything. His followers keep to themselves and meet in secret. They're afraid of the legionnaires."

"What do you think?"

"I haven't thought much about it." He sat the bowl on the ground. "I think everybody is making too much of it."

"Then you don' t think He could be the Messiah?" She was disappointed. She had hoped Nicholas might feel the same way she did - although she wasn't even sure how she felt. Why did what he believed matter to her anyway?

"What if He is? We have our gods, and they seem to take good enough care of us. Why do I need another god?"

Fearing she had offended Nicholas, and he was rebuking her, Zanah picked up the bowl and stood up. "I' m sorry. I shouldn't be here. Iona might be worried about me."

"Are you sorry you came?" He had enjoyed her visit, and kind of liked her - her openness and frankness.

"No. No, I meant I was sorry I got so involved with Jesus."

"Oh. No harm done."

"Where are you going from here?"

"We leave in the morning for Capernaum."

"Oh." She was dejected. She liked Nicholas, even if he did have enough gods without hers. She was hoping Leukas would be staying longer. "I must be going," her voice rising sharply. "Goodnight."

"Goodnight." What an engaging young woman. He watched as she ran toward the inn with the grace of a frightened deer. She disappeared in the darkness.

****

Zanah laid awake, images of Nicholas dancing in her head. She was infatuated and wanted to know more about him. Wasn't that why she went to the stable in the first place? Blaming herself for monopolizing the conversation with her inquiries about Jesus, she had learned nothing. Nicholas had obligingly told her what he knew about Jesus, but not one word about himself. She still didn't know how he became a slave, but she discerned from his manner and speech he was well educated - which was more than she could say about herself. What about his family? Where were they? Were they slaves too? What did he think of her - if anything?

Zanah realized it was foolish for her to even think about any kind of relationship with Nicholas. He was a slave. He wasn't free. He was leaving in the morning anyway. Besides, if he knew her past, he probably wouldn't even speak to her - let alone enter into a relationship with her. Still, she couldn't keep from thinking about him - and herself. What she was feeling was different than anything she had ever felt toward a man. How could this be, since she had met him only hours ago?

Zanah tossed and turned fitfully. Nicholas was leaving in the morning for Capernaum. She remembered telling Mishtar Jesus was going to Galilee. Wasn't Capernaum in Galilee? Perhaps master Leukas would let her go with them to Capernaum. She would be safe traveling with them and, when she found Jesus, she could follow Him. She had heard a great many followed Him everywhere He went. Why couldn't she follow Him too? Was this an opportunity to escape Mishtar and Gabah, and relieve Iona of any further concern for her?

The more she thought about it, the more it excited her. Not only would she be able to learn more about Jesus, but it would give her time to know Nicholas better. Which excited her most the desire to know Jesus or to know Nicholas? She wasn't sure. In spite of her emotions riding a tidal wave, she fell asleep. Zanah awoke with her mind taking up where it had left off the night before. While helping Iona, she ruminated the best way to approach master Leukas. How he would react was a matter of concern. Would he think she was a bold, brazen hussy? He might not want her tagging along, or be responsible for her. He hardly knew her. Why should he help her? Suppose he said, "No" - what then? She didn't want to think about that. She would cross that bridge when she came to it - if it came to that.

Leukas and Nicholas came in. Leukas sat at the table and Nicholas sat on a bench nearby. Pretending to be unruffled by Nicholas' presence, Zanah occasionally cast sly glances toward him. If Nicholas noticed her, or entertained similar thoughts about her, he kept it a well-guarded secret.

Spyros came in and, seating himself alongside Leukas, they resumed reminiscing old times. Zanah listened to their conversation, waiting impatiently for an opening. Breakfast lasted forever - or so it seemed. Looking at Nicholas out of the corner of her eye, Zanah was distressed - Nicholas appeared not to notice her. Leukas, arising from the table, excused himself, saying it was time they were on their way. Zanah seized the moment. It was now or never.

"Excuse me, Sir." Leukas halted; looked at her, a puzzled look on his face. Nicholas too was mystified. "May I go with you to Capernaum?"

Iona, shocked and slack-jawed, dropped the dish she was holding. "Zanah! What are you saying?" Iona asked?

Zanah explained briefly her problems with Mishtar and Gabah, and revealed her plan.

"You can' t do that!" Iona exclaimed.

"Why not?"

"Why not!? You're a Samaritan, that's why not! That's Jewish country! They'll kill you!" Leukas, Spyros and Nicholas remained silent, choosing not to enter into the argument, leaving it solely in the hands of Iona.

"I' II be safe with master Leukas, and when I find Jesus, I' II be safe with Him."

"You're out of your mind," Iona said.

"You and Spyros have been very kind to me, and I don't want to seem ungrateful, but I can' t stay here

51

forever." Turning to Leukas, who was standing there dumbfounded, not knowing what to do or say, Zanah continued. "Please, Sir. May I go with you? I promise not to cause any trouble or slow you down."

Leukas, stammering to reply, looked to Iona for help. She offered none. "If Spyros and Iona don't object, and you're sure this is what you need to do, I suppose you could go with us. But we are packed and ready to leave."

"That's all right." Zanah was bubbling with excitement. "I won't hold you up. I've already gathered up what few things I have."

Leukas looked at Iona for approval. Iona shook her head and rolled her eyes in hopeless surrender. "Go, if you must." She was well aware of the risk Zanah was taking, but she also knew Zanah was right about one thing. Her life in Sychar was at a dead end. "I hope you find what you're looking for, but if you ever want to come back, you are welcome here."

Hugging Iona, Zanah thanked her and assured her she would be all right. Bidding Spyros and Iona goodbye, the trio set out on their journey.

****

Leukas leading the way, Nicholas guiding the two laden donkeys, and Zanah bringing up the rear, they moved with caution down the narrow, rugged mountain trail. It was slow going. One careless step could plunge them headlong down the mountainside, causing severe injury - perhaps even death. Being more familiar with the trail and not being responsible for the donkeys or the cargo, the going was easier for Zanah. She permitted her mind to wander.

Marveling at Nicholas' skill in handling the donkeys, Zanah reasoned he must have made many journeys like this to have developed such skill. Everything Nicholas did caught her eye and met with tacit approval. Reaching the trade route, the going became easier and progress more rapid; for the route was heavily traveled and virtually free of obstacles.

The springs from Mount Ebal and Mount Gerizim flowed into the valley, making it one of the most fertile and productive valleys in all Samaria. Zanah had been here many times, buying fruit and vegetables for Iona, but was never impressed by it. This morning she was seeing the valley as if for the first time. Passing the vendor's stalls, she savored the aroma of fresh fruit and spices. Past the markets, the vineyards and garden patches, laid out in neat rectangular patterns, flourished. Multi-colored Lapwings darted about, emitting their shrill, wailing cry. Larks provided musical accompaniment for the pastoral scene. How beautiful and peaceful.

Walking alongside the donkeys, opposite Nicholas, Zanah reflected on recent events. Since leaving Mishtar, all be it not of her own volition, everything got better. She felt better about herself. Iona had treated her well, and she had enjoyed helping Iona. Even the encounters with Gabah weren't as bad, not that Gabah had toned down her rhetoric, but it didn't make Zanah as angry. The only thing that hadn't improved was Mishtar, and he probably never would. Now she was on her way to Galilee. Who would've thought, even as recent as yesterday, that today she would be going to Galilee.

All this had happened since meeting Jesus. Did He have anything to do with it? Zanah dismissed the idea as foolish. How could He possibly have had anything to do with it? Yet He told her all about herself, didn't He? How did He know all that? Desiring to know the answers to these questions made her more anxious than ever to see Jesus. She hoped He could explain everything.

Leaving the fertile valley, the route ascended, becoming steep and rocky. Occasionally Zanah saw flocks of sheep and goats grazing on the infrequent patches of grass. Sometimes she could hear the soft sound of a shepherd's flute off in the distance. It must be a lonesome life tending sheep and goats out here, she mused. Although the route was well traveled, they hadn't met anyone or passed anyone. They stopped to rest the donkeys, and themselves, and Leukas engaged Zanah in conversation.

"Do you have any family, Zanah?" Nicholas appeared not to be listening, pretending to check the straps securing the cargo to the donkeys.

"No, Sir. I never knew my parents."

"Someone must've raised you." Leukas offered her some raisins he took from a pouch.

"There were many someone's, Sir." Zanah said, accepting a handful of raisins. "I was passed from one family to another."

"How old were you when you struck out on your own?"

"About twelve, I guess - I'm not sure, Sir. I don't know exactly when I was born." She glanced at Nicholas to see if he was listening. He feigned disinterest, continuing to check the cargo.

"How did you manage - I mean, being so young?"

"I learned early, some men will provide for you if you provide for them, Sir." Surely Nicholas took note of that, she thought; but if he did, he gave no indication, continuing to fiddle with the cargo.

Embarrassed, Leukas apologized. "I'm sorry. I didn't mean to pry."

"It's all right, Sir. I'm not proud of my life, but I'm not ashamed either. I did what I had to do."

"Well, we better be going." Zanah and Nicholas concurred. Getting up, Leukas dusted himself off.

Back on the trail, the only sound was that of the donkey's hooves on the hard ground, and Nicholas prodding them on. Zanah resumed thinking about Nicholas, or rather what Nicholas thought about her after her conversation with master Leukas. He heard everything, she was certain, even though he pretended not to. He couldn't help hearing. What did he think of her now, or did he even entertain any thoughts about her at all? One thing was certain. He knew she was a loose woman. Surely he couldn't condemn her for what she did in the past. She was just being honest and frank with Leukas. It didn't mean she had no morals. On the other hand, what reason did she have to think Nicholas thought anything about her at all - let alone have any feelings for her. He never gave her any encouragement, but for some unexplainable reason, it was important to her that Nicholas cared.

The sun had reached its zenith, and was burning down on them by the time they reached the city of Samaria. Although the heat was sapping her strength, Zanah was excited being in the midst of so many people again. It was lonely and monotonous on the trail. The street was crowded with tents, shops and booths offering all kinds of fruits, vegetables, spices, earthenware, cloth, rugs and blankets. She had never seen such an array of merchandise in one place in her entire life. What must it be like to be able to buy some of these things? More than likely she would never find out. Roman soldiers were everywhere, which in itself was not unusual, seeing Rome kept a garrison there. Zanah was pushed, shoved and jostled constantly. Vendors, traders and buyers haggled loudly, often times profanely. Zanah felt a particularly violent jolt. She saw the perpetrator was a Roman soldier. Closer observation revealed it was Antonio. Antonio, recognizing Zanah, glared at her. Turning away from him, Zanah attached herself to Nicholas, arousing his curiosity. She watched Antonio disappear in the crowd, while Nicholas remained puzzled by Zanah's sudden closeness.

As they neared the edge of the city, the crowd thinned. Zanah welcomed the relief from the raucous throng nearly as much as she had welcomed their presence earlier. A soldier confronted them, halting their progress. It was Antonio. He didn't go on his way as Zanah assumed, but had taken another route, and now stood a menace before them.

"I have orders to arrest this woman."

"On what charge?" Leukas asked.

"I'm not at liberty to say." He reached for Zanah. "Just give me the woman, and you can be on your way."

Drawing away from Antonio, Zanah sought refuge behind Nicholas. "Don't believe him! He's lying! I haven't done anything!" Now Nicholas understood the reason for Zanah's closeness earlier. Secretly he had hoped it was something else. "Let me see your orders," Leukas demanded.

"They're verbal. Now give me the woman!" As Antonio attempted to grab Zanah, Nicholas placed himself in front of her. "Out of my way, slave!" He tried to force his way past Nicholas. Nicholas delivered a powerful blow to Antonio's jaw, dropping him to the ground. Leukas immediately urged the donkeys on. "You'll pay for this," Antonio shouted, still sitting on the ground rubbing his jaw.

As they continued on their way, Zanah was first to speak. "Thank you, Sir, for defending me." She looked at Leukas, but she was addressing Nicholas. "I never expected anything like this to happen."

"Do you know the soldier?" Leukas inquired.

"Yes, Sir. He tried to rape me while I was under his guard. I kneed him where it would hurt the most." She failed to see Nicholas stifle a grin.

"Do you think he will cause trouble?"

"No, Sir. The soldiers told me not to worry about him."

"That's good."

The sun, seeking solitary seclusion behind the mountains, meant it would soon be getting cooler, and they would be stopping for the night. Zanah, trying not to limp visibly or fall behind, needed the rest. She was tired and her feet hurt, but she refused to complain. When Leukas chose a spot a short distance off the trail and announced they would camp there for the night, noone in the party objected least of all Zanah. While Leukas gathered wood for a fire, and Nicholas tended to the donkeys and cargo, Zanah sat on a rock rubbing her aching feet.

The evening meal consisted of cracknels, raisins, nuts and wine. Shortly after the meal Leukas, covering himself with a heavy robe, laid down by the fire and went to sleep. Nicholas remained seated on a boulder a short distance from the fire. Zanah joined him.

"Thanks for saving me from that soldier."

"It was nothing."

"It was to me. Nobody ever defended me before." Picking up a small stone, she toyed with it, tossing it up and catching it.

"I'm happy I could be of service."

"Damned Nicholas' formal attitude," Zanah muttered under her breath as she threw the stone on the ground with emphasis. She wanted him to be more friendly, perhaps even intimate.

"Master Leukas asked if I had any family," Zanah said, regaining her composure. "May I ask you the same thing? Do you have any family?"

"No, my parents were both killed by robbers."

"I'm sorry," Zanah said.

"They would have killed me too except they figured I was worth more on the slave market."

Zanah was happy Nicholas was loosening up and becoming more casual and talkative; though he remained somewhat aloof. "That's how you became a slave?"

"They took me to Alexandria and put me on the block."

"And master Leukas bought you?" Zanah's attention was riveted on Nicholas, and she saw the hurt in his eyes. She wanted to embrace him and offer words of comfort, but she refrained.

"Yes. He happened to be there and recognized me - he knew my family. He bid on me to save me from becoming a slave to anyone else. He paid a terribly high price for me."

"Why didn't he set you free after that?"

"He wanted to, but I insisted on serving him until I paid my debt."

"That was very commendable."

"Not really. He saved my life. What's a human life worth? What's your life worth? What would you give for your life?"

"I never thought of it like that."

It's getting late," Nicholas said, snapping out of his melancholy. "We have a long day ahead of us. We better get some rest."

"Yes, I am tired." Zanah laid her hand on his. "Thank you for telling me about your family." She noticed he didn't pull his hand away. "Good night," she said. Nicholas smiled. She got up and walked over near the fire.

Wrapped in her blanket, Zanah watched the embers of the fire glow bright, fade and glow bright again with each puff of wind. She mulled over what Nicholas had told her. So that's how he became a slave, and why Leukas doesn't treat him like one. It must have been a terrifying experience, losing your parents and being carried off to a strange country. She wondered how old he was when all this happened, and how much longer before master Leukas would be paid in full.

Zanah recalled when she laid her hand on his, he didn't pull his hand away. Was he beginning to care about her? Did he have feelings for her? He defended her at considerable risk to himself, didn't he? That ought to mean something - even if the soldier was only Antonio. Was Nicholas holding back because he was a slave indebted to master Leukas, and didn't have anything to offer a woman? Yes, that must be what it was. Nicholas did care for her. With that thought dancing in her head, she fell asleep.

****

Zanah awoke to see Leukas putting out the last embers of the fire, and Nicholas replacing the load back on the donkeys. She heard Leukas tell Nicholas they would travel for an hour or two before eating. She wasn't sure if it was the night's rest, although that surely helped, or the renewed hope that Nicholas cared, but her feet didn't hurt anymore and she felt as frisky as a young colt. She preferred to credit Nicholas.

Nicholas had asked her, "What's your life worth?" Not much, she reckoned. If something happened to her, who would know it? Who would even miss her? What would she give for her life? There were times she wouldn't have given a penny for it. In fact she thought about doing herself in - for free. But now her life was increasing in value with each passing day.

About the third hour they stopped to rest and eat. Leukas broke out some bread, fruit and cheese he had purchased while in Samaria. Food tasted exceptionally good to Zanah this morning. Everything was good. Even the barren, rock-covered mountains looked good. How good everything is has a lot to do with one's attitude, Zanah concluded. She glanced at Nicholas, and his eyes met hers. He smiled. Zanah's heart nearly leaped out of her chest.

Their repast was interrupted by a lone traveler on a donkey. Zanah perceived he was not a trader, the donkey bearing no burden except for the man - which in itself was unusual. Most people walked, not being able to afford a donkey just to ride. When he dismounted, she saw he had a noticeable limp - which she surmised was why he rode the donkey. It would be difficult for him to walk any distance. He introduced himself as Silas - no last name. Leukas introduced the three of them and invited him to join them - which, without hesitation, he accepted.

"Where you from?" Leukas asked, handing Silas some bread and cheese.

"Magdala; and you, Sir?" The mention of Magdala made Zanah perk up her ears. She knew Magdala was in Galilee.

"Nicholas and I are from Alexandria, and Zanah is from Sychar."

Leukas and Silas engaged in small talk - neither Nicholas nor Zanah entering into it. Zanah wanted to question Silas about Galilee, especially about Jesus. With difficulty she managed to control her anxiety. At length, Silas announced he must be on his way, and mounted his donkey.

"Sir," Zanah said. "You said you were from Galilee. Do you know a Galilean named Jesus?"

"Everybody in Galilee knows Jesus."

"Tell me about Him, Sir."

Saying there wasn't time enough to tell everything, Silas related how Jesus, followed by His disciples and crowds of people, went from village to village preaching repentance and the kingdom of God, and performing miracles. Silas told about Jesus changing water into wine at a marriage feast in Cana, and healing a rich man's son. Silas said Jesus healed many people and cast out demon spirits.

"Did you see Him do any of those things?" Leukas asked."

"No, Sir."

"Then what you're telling us is only hearsay."

"Yes, Sir, you might say that. I didn' t see Him do any of those things, but I was paralyzed and Jesus healed me, not completely, but it was enough." Digging his heels into the donkey's flanks, Silas started down the trail, leaving the three of them standing in awkward silence.

Zanah, noting Leukas' skepticism, assumed Nicholas felt the same way. Did Silas change their opinion? As for her, it whetted her desire to know more about Jesus.

By the eleventh hour they emerged from the barren mountains of Samaria, and gazed upon the fruitful

Plain of Esdraelon in Galilee. Zanah gasped in wonder. The view was breathtaking. The valley at Shechem, as bountiful as it was, couldn't compare with the Plain of Esdraelon. Green rolling hills, fields of grain like a sea of waving gold, the snow-capped Lebanese mountains looming in the background - awesome. Zanah pinched herself to make sure she wasn't dreaming. Leukas announced they would spend the night here. He set out food for their evening meal while Nicholas tended the donkeys and Zanah gathered firewood.

"By this time tomorrow we should be in Capernaum," Leukas said, pouring the wine. He expected Zanah to make some comment or show some emotion, but she did neither; prompting Leukas to question her. "What are you thinking about, Zanah?"

"I was thinking about that man, Silas."

"What about him?" Leukas took a sip of wine and passed the cheese around.

"Did you believe him, Sir?" She accepted the cheese.

"No reason not to, but what you really want to know is, do I believe Jesus healed him."

"Yes, I guess so." She held the cheese in her hand, but didn't eat.

"No. No, I don't." Leukas said, stuffing a morsel of cheese in his mouth and washing it down with a swallow of wine.

"Then how do you explain it, Sir?" She noticed Nicholas paying close attention, but not offering any comment.

"I don't. Probably some quirk of nature or fate."

Finishing his meal, Leukas retreated a short distance, leaving Zanah and Nicholas alone. Zanah hoped she hadn't offended Leukas with her constant talking about Jesus. Leukas was good to her, and she didn't want to spoil their relationship. She wondered if Nicholas too might be getting tired of hearing about Jesus. She certainly didn't want to alienate him - especially now that she knew he was beginning to care.

"How long are you and master Leukas staying in Capernaum?" Zanah asked Nicholas, who was putting up what was left after their meal.

"He hasn't said, but probably not more than a day or two."

"Where are you going then?"

"Caesarea and then Alexandria. What about you?"

"I don't have any plans except finding Jesus." Why did the conversation always lead to Jesus? She hated it. Not that she didn't want to talk about Jesus, but why couldn't she talk about other things - like Nicholas? Jesus was invading her whole life.

"Then what?" Nicholas asked, unmindful of Zanah's frustration.

"Who knows," Zanah said, shrugging her shoulders.

"I don't understand your obsession with Jesus," Nicholas said, out of confusion more than irritation.

"I don't understand it either. It's just something I feel I have to do. Haven't you ever felt like there was something you just had to do?" Nicholas ignored her question.

"Would you consider going to Alexandria with us?" Seeing the look of surprise on Zanah's face, he realized how inappropriate his question was. He had only extended vague hints that he was interested in her, let alone weighing the feasibility of taking her with him. She was struggling to reply. "I'm sorry," Nicholas went on. "I was out of line."

"No, no - it's all right. It just took me by surprise."

"Then you will go with us?" There was eager anticipation in his voice.

"I'm sorry, Nicholas. As much as I want to, I - I can't."

"Can' t or won' t?"

Zanah saw the hurt in Nicholas' eyes - the same hurt she saw when he talked about his parents. Why did she respond the way she did? Ever since she laid eyes on him, she had hoped he would care about her; and now that he expressed his desire for her, she turned him down. For what? To go on a wild goose chase? She couldn't bear to talk about it anymore. Excusing herself, she took her blanket and laid down. Sleep was impossible. Her beautiful world came crashing down far more rapidly than it had risen. She remembered the sleepless night at the inn when she plotted and schemed to accompany Leukas to Capernaum. Then she was too excited to sleep. Now the conflict raging within her - Nicholas or Jesus - was keeping her awake.

As Leukas made preparation the next morning for continuing their journey, he noticed Nicholas and Zanah avoiding each other. He thought he had observed a relationship developing. Something must have come between them, he reasoned, but what? He decided against intervening.

Were it not for the coolness between Zanah and Nicholas, this leg of the journey would be the most pleasant because of the ease of travel and interesting scenery. As it was, the strain affected everyone, making them short-tempered and irritable. At the small village of Nain, Leukas decided it was time to stop and eat - seeing it was the third hour.

Nain was a lot like Sychar, Zanah observed, only not as mountainous and rocky. It was about the same size, but the houses were made of mud bricks instead of limestone - making them look dark and shabby - and the roofs were made of straw. Resuming their journey, they came upon a group of men involved in a loud, animated discussion. They did not appear to be arguing, but were obviously excited about something. Leukas would have passed them by except he heard enough of their conversation to cause him to stop and inquire further. Scrutinizing Leukas, one of the men, who seemed to be the authority for the group, explained.

"We were carrying the body of a widow's only son for burial outside the village, when Jesus came along. Jesus said to the widow, "Don't cry." Then He went up and touched the coffin and said, "Young man, I say to you get up." The dead man sat up and talked."

"When did this happen?" Leukas asked.

"Only yesterday. Everyone was filled with awe. They all said, "A great prophet is among us. God has come to help his people.""

Zanah's pulse quickened, and she spoke without considering her station as a woman and a Samaritan. "Where does this widow live? Can we talk to her?"

"That is not possible," the authority said. "Because of the press of the people and curiosity seekers, the son has taken his mother, and they are in seclusion somewhere - noone knows where." Leukas thanked the

73

man, and they continued on to a place where they stopped to rest. Discussing the event, Leukas remained skeptical. They were always hearing about these miracles, but never able to speak to anyone who received the miracle - like the widow's son. Zanah assumed Leukas had either forgotten about Silas, or dismissed it as not being a miracle.

Leukas theorized the son wasn't dead, only unconscious or in a coma. By the time the funeral procession reached the edge of the village, he regained consciousness. Jesus happened to come along at that time. "Simple as that," Leukas said. "Besides," Leukas noted, "Jews were an excitable, superstitious people anyway." Nicholas did not volunteer an opinion, nor did he dispute Leukas' theory. Zanah, her spirit somewhat crushed by Leukas continual skepticism, thought it best not to enter her opinion - seeing her relationship with Nicholas and Leukas was already strained. She still believed Jesus was special and did those things, and was more determined than ever to find Him. Continuing their journey, they passed expediently through the villages of Magdala and

Tabigha, there being no further incidents to hinder them. Neither village impressed Zanah, for they contributed nothing toward the beauty of the countryside or stimulated her appetite concerning Jesus. Walking the same road she knew Jesus walked, Zanah felt something akin to awe - or was it reverence? It was as if Jesus was walking by her side instead of Leukas and Nicholas. The presence of an increasing number of Roman soldiers brought Antonio to her mind. Although none were Antonio, the possibility unnerved her. The nearer they got to Capernaum, the more crowded the highway became.

It was the tenth hour when they approached the city. Zanah noticed two large, stone lions, assisted by a legionnaire, guarding the entrance to the city. The legionnaire ordered them to join a long line of people waiting to pay duty on their goods to the tax collector. A lengthy wait ensued before they reached the tax collector's table, and Leukas declared the goods he was bringing in. After considerable dickering and capitulation, Leukas agreed to and paid the specified duty, and they entered the city.

Zanah appreciated master Leukas' expertise in handling affairs. When she decided to go to Galilee, she never considered having to deal with things like customs and tax collectors. She could never handle that. Of course she didn't have any money or anything to declare either. Though the hour was late, the streets were still teeming with merchants and peddlers - some carrying their wares on their back. They passed rows of stalls and booths selling clothing, pottery, fruit, nuts and fish - the latter emitting an odor that caused Zanah to hold her nose and quicken her steps. As was the case in Samaria, they were pushed and shoved by people from every walk of life and every part of the world - but it seemed worse here. Gawking at all the sights, Zanah momentarily forgot she was with Leukas and Nicholas, becoming separated from them, and having to hurry to catch up. Leaving the shops and market behind, they stopped at an inn where, Leukas informed them, they would spend the night. Since Leukas couldn't deliver his merchandise until morning, Nicholas was required to stay in the stable guarding it. Leukas intended to obtain a room for Zanah, but she asked permission to stay with Nicholas, a request that caused Nicholas to raise his eyebrows, surprised.

"Why?" Leukas asked.

"It's a personal matter. Please, Sir."

Leukas looked at Nicholas for some sign of approval or disapproval, but saw Nicholas was as mystified as he was. With reluctance, Leukas granted Zanah's request. Whatever Zanah's motive was, Leukas figured Nicholas had as much right to a life as anyone. Nicholas, leading the donkeys, set out for the stable, Zanah by his side.

"Why do you want to sleep in the stable?" Nicholas asked.

"Can't you guess? Nicholas, I want to be with you, and I want to apologize."

Nicholas stopped short. "Apologize? What for?"

"For the way I bungled your invitation." They resumed walking toward the stable. "I'm sorry I hurt you."

"No, I am to blame. I had no right to make such an offer."

"I'm glad you did," Zanah said, reaching the stable. Nicholas began unloading the donkeys. Zanah helped him loosen the straps. "I do want to go with you."

"You've decided to go?" He stopped with the unloading, and turned to Zanah. She saw the delight in his face.

"Please try to understand. I want to, but until I get over this passion I have for Jesus - I don't mean in a romantic way - it wouldn't be fair to you. There would always be this unrequited wanting standing between us."

"From what I've heard, I can see how a person might get caught up in Him." Nicholas resumed the unloading. "He seems to be a very unique person."

"Yes, very unique." She watched as Nicholas finished the unloading, and began feeding the donkeys. "Let's not talk about Jesus anymore." Her voice was cheerful. "So, you and master Leukas will deliver your merchandise in the morning?"

"What will you do?"

"I've heard Jesus is often seen by the sea. I guess I will go there."

"Will you come back here?"

"I don't know. It depends on whether…"

"You find Jesus or not?" Zanah didn't reply. Nicholas took hold of Zanah's hands and looked into her eyes. There was an air of pleading in his voice. "I don't understand what it is you are seeking, but I don't want to risk losing you. Zanah, I love you." Zanah's pulse quickened sending a shudder of emotion surging through her body.

"Oh, Nicholas, I can' t begin to tell you how much I have wanted to hear you say that. I love you too, but what can we do?"

"What do you mean?"

"I mean, in a way, neither of us is free."

"I'm sure master Leukas would allow us to be together."

"But I'm not free. I'm more enslaved than you are."

"Will you ever be free from Jesus?"

"I believe once I find Him and know the truth, I will be free."

"Then I will wait for you."

"You are willing to wait for me?" Zanah hugged Nicholas. It was more than she dared expect - someone caring enough for her they were willing to wait.

"I will wait if you promise to be faithful, and come to me as soon as you are free."

"How will I know where you are?"

"Master Leukas has a permanent home in Alexandria. Sooner or later we always return to it. You can write to me there. I'll write to you in care of Spyros' inn. Will you promise?"

"I promise." She hoped Nicholas would seal their promise by making love to her. She was willing - no, eager - to submit to him, although she knew this wasn't the proper place. Who cares when you're in love? Nicholas, making no advances however, was content to let the matter rest.

"We better get some rest. Tomorrow will be a busy day for both of us," Nicholas said.

"All right. Goodnight. I love you."

"I love you too, Zanah." He kissed her on her lips, long and passionate. "Goodnight."

The commitment she made kept her awake - not that she regretted making it, or doubted her resolve to keep it - but she was wound so tight with emotion, sleep was impossible. For several minutes she just laid there looking at Nicholas, already asleep. He looked so handsome and peaceful. Allowing her mind to roam free, she conjured up ecstatic visions of life with Nicholas. Yes, she made the right decision. Convinced that once she found Jesus and learned the truth, her obsession would be satiated, and she would be free to be with Nicholas. She might even be able to find the truth before master Leukas and Nicholas left Capernaum. With that, she fell asleep.

****

Joining Nicholas and Zanah, Leukas noticed the coldness between the two no longer existed. He suspected what might have gone on in the stable, and couldn't help grinning. He guessed he did the right thing. He felt good about having let Zanah spend the night with Nicholas. Everything in order, Leukas suggested they be about their business. Nicholas, with the donkeys loaded and in tow, started to move out.

"I'm not going," Zanah said.

"Not going!" Leukas stopped short, scowling at Zanah.

"I only asked to go with you to Capernaum, Sir. I don't want to seem ungrateful, but I'm here now, and it's time for me to go my way."

"Which is?"

"To find Jesus."

"And where do you propose looking for Him?"

"I told Nicholas Jesus is often seen by the sea. I plan to start there."

"And then what?" Leukas asked. Zanah shrugged her shoulders as if to say, "Who knows." Leukas continued, "I can't let you go wandering off by yourself. I hear this Jesus is becoming quite unpopular - especially with Rome. You could be putting yourself in grave danger." Leukas spoke as much out of concern for Nicholas as for Zanah. He wanted Nicholas to have a home of his own, a wife and family.

If Zanah was Nicholas' choice, then he wanted to save her from herself - if he could.

"I' ll be all right, Sir," Zanah protested.

"Nonsense! If you insist on going ahead with this foolishness, I'm sending Nicholas with you." In his heart, he hoped they wouldn't find Jesus, Zanah would give up this obsession and return with Nicholas.

"Please, Sir. You need Nicholas to help you."

"I can handle it myself." He turned to Nicholas. "Nicholas, do as I say. That's an order." He took the lines from Nicholas. "And don't let anything happen to her." He gave Nicholas a wink.

"Yes, Sir." Nicholas welcomed the opportunity to be with Zanah. Catching Leukas' wink, he wondered if Leukas suspected there was something between him and Zanah. It was out of character for Leukas to give him time off when there was work to be done. Nicholas' desire was that the added time together would encourage Zanah to change her mind.

With Nicholas by her side, Zanah relaxed and enjoyed the sights. She noticed the Greek influence was strong throughout the city even though Capernaum was primarily Jewish, and Greek rule ended long ago. The city was laid out in square blocks - a Greek custom. Most of the buildings and houses were made from black basalt stone - some whitewashed to make them more attractive.

They passed the synagogue, an imposing structure made of limestone and marble. It stood two stories high, its gleaming marble columns leading into a courtyard. It was evident to Zanah the Romans had a vital interest in the city, for Roman legionnaires were everywhere, and a Roman fort was in nearby Tiberias. She noticed a steady stream of people on the highway leading to Bethsaida, causing her to wonder why so many people were going in that direction.

The local scene wasn't all that appealed to Zanah. Walking alongside Nicholas, she felt ten cubits tall, and without a care in the world. She tried picturing what it would be like walking beside Nicholas the rest of her life. How much longer did he have to work before master Leukas gave him his manumission? Then what would Nicholas do for a living? He wouldn't be like Mishtar and do nothing, that was for sure. Would he continue traveling with master Leukas, leaving her alone in Alexandria? That didn't appeal to her. Still lost in thought, they arrived by the Sea of Galilee.

Fishing boats were lined up along the shoreline, their nets hanging out to dry; but the entire shoreline was deserted except for a lone fisherman mending a net. They approached him and engaged him in conversation - which proved to be one-sided, the fisherman being apprehensive of them. A lone woman accompanied by a slave was not a common sight. Between grunts and looks of suspicion and wariness, he answered their queries in the fewest words possible.

Convincing the fisherman they were not seeking Jesus to do Him harm, he informed them everyone had gone to Bethsaida to see Jesus in the hope of seeing a miracle or being healed of some malady. "It's been that way the past two days," the fisherman told them. Zanah recalled noticing the stream of people headed toward Bethsaida. "So that's where everyone was going," she said under her breath. Bethsaida, being less than an hour's walk from where they were, they decided to go there.

Finding Jesus in a village the size of Bethsaida was not difficult - considering the size crowds Jesus attracted. They found Him seated on the slope of a grassy hill, His disciples seated around Him. Zanah counted them. There were twelve. Zanah and Nicholas edged their way through the crowd to get a better view. People kept bringing their sick, blind and lame, and Jesus healed them all - not partially like Silas claimed, but completely. Zanah stared in amazement. Between acts of healing, Jesus taught about the kingdom of God - urging everyone to repent and be baptized for the remission of sin. Zanah, engrossed in what was happening, as were others in the crowd, failed to notice the sun had settled behind the hills, and it was getting dark. Zanah heard the disciples press Jesus to send the people away, for it was late, they were hungry, and they didn't have enough food to feed everyone. Jesus rejected their suggestion. One of the disciples handed Jesus what looked to her like four or five biscuits and two small fish he had received from a small boy.

"How far will that go among so many?" one disciple scoffed. Zanah watched as Jesus prayed, broke the bread and fish into pieces, and told the disciples to have the people sit down. Then Jesus distributed the bread to those who were seated - as much as they wanted. He did the same with the fish. When they all had enough to eat, Jesus told the disciples to gather the pieces that were left over. Zanah watched dumbfounded as the disciples gathered the leftovers. They gathered far more than there was to begin with - twelve baskets full to be exact. She counted them. Nicholas also took notice of the strange phenomena. Would it change his opinion of Jesus? She hoped so. Nicholas decided it was time they returned to Capernaum.

Returning to the inn, Zanah and Nicholas learned Leukas had delivered the merchandise and, having no further use for the donkeys, had sold them. He also took the liberty of obtaining separate rooms at the inn for Nicholas and Zanah.

The inn was much larger and more elaborate than Spyros' inn, consisting of four large buildings surrounding a courtyard - each building containing three or four separate rooms. Opposite the entrance to the courtyard was the main building, housing the owner's quarters as well as the public dining area. Leukas reserved one of the three-room buildings, providing a private room for each of them.

Zanah and Nicholas told Leukas about the miracles they had witnessed, Leukas remaining unimpressed in spite of Zanah's enthusiasm. Zanah decided that, the older one gets, the harder it is for them to change or accept new ideas. Nicholas, although impressed by what he saw, was more subdued. Like Leukas, he was not fully convinced it was legitimate, and not magic or sleight of hand; but he also witnessed how Zanah got caught up in it. It helped him better understand her obsession.

Leukas pointed out the miracles were probably rigged. The sick and lame only pretended to be sick and lame. As for feeding so many people on such meager rations, Leukas rationalized that by saying they must have obtained more food while Zanah and Nicholas were distracted. Zanah remained convinced

Jesus performed the miracles, but chose not to dispute the matter with Leukas.

Before retiring, Leukas informed Nicholas they would leave for Caesarea at sun-up.

"Master Leukas seems to think I'm going with you," Zanah said, as she and Nicholas strolled in the courtyard.

"I hoped you might change your mind," Nicholas said, seating himself on a marble bench. The still air was heavy with the sweet smell of Anemone. It reminded Zanah of a funeral. She could hear a dog barking in the distance - probably at the moon or something stirring that it didn't think should be there - a hare or rat perhaps. An owl seeking its nightly meal added its doleful hoot. Zanah sat on the bench alongside Nicholas. "My heart wants to go with you, and it will; but my conscience tells me to finish what I've started."

"How will you know when its finished?" Nicholas put his arm around Zanah and drew her close.

"I'll know. I don't know how, but I'll know." She snuggled up to him.

"I hope it won't be too long. I'll worry about you."

"Nobody ever worried about me before." She snuggled even closer. "I love you for it."

"I have cause for concern. This is a dangerous thing you're doing."

"I'll be all right. Something just tells me I will. I can' t explain it."

"Be sure to let me know how you are doing."

"You too."

Nicholas kissed her long and hard, and the blood ran hot through her body.

"It's getting late. We better go in," Nicholas said, getting up from the bench. He extended his hand to Zanah. They walked hand in hand to Zanah's room. Nicholas paused. Taking her in his arms he asked, "Will you stay with me tonight? Zanah didn't answer, but followed him to his room.

****

Zanah and Nicholas were up before Leukas. She thought it would be better if she left before Leukas came - preventing further discussion and argument. Nicholas reluctantly agreed.

Pledging their love and promising to keep each other informed, they embraced, stole one last kiss and Zanah left the inn.

Nicholas watched until she was out of sight, Leukas interrupting his vigil.

"Where's Zanah?"

"She's gone."

"Gone? Gone where?"

"Wherever it is she has to go to find what she's looking for."

"You love her, don't you?"

"Yes, Sir."

"Then why did you let her go?"

"I had to. We could never be happy as long as she has this passion for Jesus."

"Do you want to go with her? You don't have to stay with me, you know."

"No. No, she promised to come to me when she's found whatever it is she's looking for."

"Suppose she never finds it, or worse yet, suppose Jesus Himself comes between you. Have you thought about that?"

"The attraction isn't romantic, or even emotional. I don't know how to describe it. It's more..." Nicholas paused, groping for the right word. "It's more mystical, or spiritual."

"Son," Leukas said, placing his hand on Nicholas' shoulder. The form of address snapped Nicholas out of his lethargy. Leukas had never called him, "Son." It never occurred to Nicholas that Leukas thought of him as his son. Come to think of it, Leukas never married or had any children. Nicholas guessed Leukas saw him as the son he never had. Why hadn't he observed this before?

Leukas continued, "I hope it works out for you."

"Thank you, Sir. I believe it will."

"When we get to Alexandria, I'm giving you a certificate of manumission. You will be free to go wherever you choose."

"That's very kind of you, Sir, but I choose to stay with you."

"Then you'll stay with me as a partner, not a slave."

"You're very generous, Sir. It's more than I deserve."

"Nonsense! You've earned it, and you deserve it." He embraced Nicholas. "We better be on our way. I've arranged to lead a small caravan to Caesarea."

The journey proved uneventful as the highway from Capernaum to Caesarea was well traveled, offering few obstacles. Nearly half the journey was over the rolling hills of southern Galilee and across the Plain of Esdraelon. The biggest problem was keeping the members of the caravan close together and prodding the stragglers on. Nicholas proved exceptionally helpful in dealing with the animals, especially the camels, which were frequently stubborn and mean spirited.

Arriving at Caesarea, Leukas found the ship ready and waiting. All that remained to be done was supervise loading the goods from the caravan onto the ship. It gave Nicholas time to dash off a short note to Zanah, telling her about Leukas giving him his freedom and making him a partner. He closed the note expressing his love and renewing his pledge to wait for her. He addressed the note to Zanah in care of Spyros' inn at Sychar, and gave it to a trader going that way. That accomplished, Leukas and Nicholas boarded the ship and were underway.

Chapter Three

Leaving Nicholas, Zanah, afraid of losing her resolve to find Jesus, didn't dare look back. She failed to foresee how difficult leaving Nicholas would be. Having had five husbands, living with Mishtar and her brushes with Gabah were like another life - another person. She couldn't picture living that way now. What happened to change her attitude and nature? Was it Jesus, Iona, Nicholas; or a combination of all three? Whatever it was, Zanah welcomed the change. She was happy and in love. Life wasn't one horrible experience after another. She had something to look forward to - a purpose, hope. Just thinking about it gave her renewed vigor and vitality. She went to the hillside outside Bethsaida where she had last seen Jesus.

At the hillside, Zanah saw a number of people milling around, undoubtedly hoping to see Jesus or a miracle, but Jesus wasn't there. Seeing a woman who looked to be about her own age, Zanah approached her to inquire about Jesus. Another woman, Zanah reasoned, would be more accommodating than a man - and less risky. From her features, Zanah saw the woman wasn't a Jewess. The material and cut of her clothing told Zanah she was poor. Her long black hair framed a thin face, heavy dark eyebrows and brown eyes. She looked frail, as if suffering from some kind of sickness or disease - which likely accounted for her being here. Like so many others, she was seeking healing. In spite of her appearance, she seemed happy, even jovial. Zanah wondered what she was doing here alone, and then thought about herself. "What am I doing here alone?"

"Excuse me," Zanah said. "Do you know where Jesus is?"

The woman eyed Zanah with suspicion. Why did everyone go on the defensive when asked about Jesus? The fisherman had refused to talk to her and Nicholas until he was convinced they meant no harm; and now this woman was equally wary. Why so cautious? After all, Jesus appeared openly before hundreds, even thousands. Why was everyone she asked so evasive?

"What do you want with Him?"

"I was here yesterday when Jesus fed everyone and talked about the kingdom of God. I want to know more about Jesus and His kingdom."

Satisfied with Zanah's explanation, the woman relaxed and talked freely, even smiling. Zanah saw she was quite pretty when she smiled. "I don't know where He is. Some people said they saw Him get in a boat and go across the sea."

"Will He be back?"

"Oh, yes, I'm sure He will."

"How can you be so sure?"

"He always has. He takes short trips throughout Galilee and Phoenicia, but He always comes back here. He stays at Simon Peter's house."

"You seem to know a lot about Him."

"I should," the woman said, brushing her long black hair from her face. "I was possessed by demons, and He cast them out." Zanah gasped, putting her hand over her mouth. She was talking to someone Jesus had healed.

"Tell me about it, please!" Zanah pleaded, moving closer to the woman, as if expecting her to reveal some secret, confidential information.

"Truthfully, I don't know much about it. My mother is Syro-Phoenician," she said, confirming Zanah's conclusion she was not a Jewess. "She told me that, on one of Jesus' visits to Phoenicia, she asked Him to cast out the demons. She heard He had cast out demons from others, and believed He could cast out mine."

"And He did!" Zanah exclaimed, her brown eyes flashing with excitement.

"Not at first. Jesus told my mother she wasn't a Jew, and He had come to the house of Israel first. My mother pleaded with Him until He obliged her."

"Wonderful! Amazing! Absolutely wonderful and amazing!" Zanah exclaimed, jumping up and down, clapping her hands with glee.

"Do you believe in Jesus?" the woman asked, smiling at Zanah's outburst.

"I, I don't know," Zanah stammered. "I only talked to Him one time." Her countenance brightened. It occurred to her she and the woman had something in common, seeing neither of them were Jews. "But ever since then, my life has been different," she confided.

"Did He heal you of some sickness?"

"No, not that I know of, but something about Him has drawn me to Him. I can' t explain it. I need some answers."

"You think He can provide you with the answers?"

"If He can't, then nobody can."

"That's why I'm here too. I'm seeking some answers." Extending her hand to Zanah she said, "I' m Rea."

"I'm Zanah," she said, taking Rea's hand.

They strolled down the hill toward the highway leading to Capernaum. Rea spoke first.

"Where are you staying?"

"I don't have any place."

"You can stay with me."

"That's very kind of you."

"Wait 'til you see where I live. You won't think I'm so kind." Rea laughed. "You may not want to stay."

"It can't be any worse than sleeping on the ground under the stars. Besides, I'm not used to much." Rea's carefree attitude was infectious, and Zanah laughed with delight.

"Then it's settled."

They ambled toward Capernaum, babbling like school girls, sharing stories and experiences from their respective lives. Except for Iona, Zanah never had any female companions, and you really couldn't call Iona a companion. Zanah's entire life had been dominated by men, most of them of questionable character, like Mishtar. Nicholas was the only man she knew who was morally honest and sincere, except Spyros and master Leukas of course - but they didn't count as men in her life.

Zanah liked Rea. She was a delightful, free-spirited woman, vivacious and garrulous. Zanah wondered what Rea was like when she was demon possessed. What a wonderful thing Jesus did for Rea, and for her mother. Zanah was curious about Rea's mother, and why Rea left home. Then she recalled Rea saying she wanted to know more about Jesus. Rea had asked

Zanah if Jesus healed her of some sickness, and she had answered, "No, not that I know of." Yet her life was changed, and not just her life, but her attitude and nature. Did Jesus in some miraculous way heal her of her adulterous, sinful ways?

Along the way, Rea explained why everyone was reluctant to talk about Jesus or reveal His whereabouts. Jesus' popularity was creating enemies. There were those, especially the rulers of the synagogue and priests, who wanted Him killed. Pilate's concern was the kingdom Jesus kept talking about. He was afraid Jesus would stir up a rebellion against Rome, thus making his position more difficult. Pilate ordered soldiers to break up any group they thought were followers of Jesus. Some were thrown in prison. People were justifiably fearful for Jesus and for themselves, especially the poor people who made up most of Jesus' followers. Jesus, it seems, was the only one who wasn't afraid. He knew what people were saying, and that the Jews were plotting against Him; but He continued teaching and healing as if it was of no consequence. Jesus kept saying, "My time has not come," - whatever that meant.

Rea was right when she said her place wasn't much. Zanah saw a square, flat-roofed, black basalt house with a single room, sparsely furnished. It reminded her of Mishtar's house, except his was better furnished. Rea's house contained a low, wooden table and a wooden bench. That was all. A couple of goatskins on the floor alongside the table were for reclining and sleeping on. A hole surrounded by stones in the center of the dirt floor served as a fireplace for heating and cooking - which Zanah perceived Rea did very little of. Rea lived alone. Zanah wondered how she subsisted. In fact, the thought came to her, how was she going to subsist? Any worries or concerns Zanah had were dispelled by Rea's warmth and light-heartedness. If Rea wasn't concerned, why should she be? Zanah appreciated having a friend and a place to stay - such as it was.

Zanah built a fire, lighting the room with a soft, orange flickering glow, hiding the barrenness and ugliness of the room. Noting the hour was past the first watch, Zanah settled down on one of the goatskins for the night. Rea laid down on the other one. Happy and relaxed, Zanah dozed off. A short time later a sound, or a feeling - Zanah didn't know which - aroused her. She saw by the flickering light, Rea was gone. Getting up, Zanah went outside, thinking Rea, perhaps unable to sleep, had gone outside for some fresh air. She wasn't outside. Where could she be? It worried Zanah, and she was fitful and restless throughout the night. Each time she woke up, she looked to see if Rea had returned. She had not.

The early morning sounds of the city coming to life - carts rattling, wheels squeaking, men shouting at donkeys, camels and each other, hooves clopping - awakened Zanah. Rea, bright and cheerful, came in.

"Where have you been?" Zanah asked. "I've been worried about you."

"I'm sorry. I didn't mean to worry you."

"Where did you go?"

"To the inn."

"The inn! Why?" No sooner had Zanah asked than the answer came to her. The scenario was a familiar one. She had often done the same thing in order to have a place to sleep or something to eat. Zanah understood Rea's circumstance, but the reality made her gasp. "Oh, no!"

"We have to eat," Rea said, as if the end justified the means.

"I can't let you do that. I can't let you support me that way, and I'm not going to do the same."

"What else can we do?"

"I don't know, but we'll think of something. I don't believe Jesus cast the demons out of you just so you could prostitute yourself. There must be a better way." Her sermonizing amazed Zanah. There was a time, not too many years ago, she would have been at the inn with Rea. The change in her outlook and morals continued to mystify her. It wasn't something she consciously and willingly tried to change, but they had changed.

****

Zanah and Rea walked down to the Sea of Galilee, chattering like chipmunks as they went. The air was fresh and clean. Sparrows chirped incessantly. Wild flowers tossed their heads to and fro, propelled by a wisp of a breeze, and emitted a sweet aroma. Spring was in the air, and Zanah's thoughts turned to love - meaning Nicholas. Where was he, and what was he doing, she wondered? Did he think about her? Nicholas was never far removed from her mind. She never mentioned Nicholas to Rea - no need to. Rea never spoke of any love interest, so the subject never came up. They managed to find enough other things to talk about.

Fishermen were coming in with their night's catch. Zanah saw some had done only fair, others poorly or nothing at all. Fishing, like everything else, Zanah reasoned, required skill and knowledge plus a lot of luck - not to mention a strong back. She recognized four of the fishermen, particularly the big one, as having been with Jesus at Bethsaida. He stood out from the others, and acted like he was the leader. At least he was the most talkative. Rea said he was Simon Peter. She thought the other three were Andrew, Philip and John, but she wasn't sure. Their boat was one that had fared poorly. In fact, they had caught nothing.

As if He popped up out of the ground, or dropped down out of the sky, Jesus appeared. He got into the boat, and Zanah heard Him tell Peter to put out a little from the shore. Then Jesus, from His place in the boat, taught those gathered on the shore. When He finished speaking, He told Peter to launch out into the deep water, and let down the net. Peter protested so loudly Zanah and everyone else heard him - complaining they had worked hard all night and hadn't caught anything. Even so, Peter let down the net. The net filled with so many fish it was about to sink the boat - if it didn't break first. Peter cried out to the other fishermen for help. Zanah, caught up in the drama, waded out to help, only to find herself floundering in deep water. Returning to Rea, soaked to the skin, she felt foolish. Rea laughed. Overcoming her embarrassment, Zanah joined her. They laughed until their sides ached.

When they got back to the house, Zanah stripped off her wet clothes and wrapped herself in a robe belonging to Rea. Laying her wet clothes on the grass to dry, Zanah and Rea sat outside, basking in the warm sunshine.

"The Feast of the Passover is next week," Rea said, stretching cat-like in the sun. "Jesus will be going to Jerusalem."

"Why don't we go?" Zanah asked.

"Do you realize what you're suggesting?" Rea asked, sitting up.

"Why? What's wrong with that?"

"We can't go to Jerusalem for the Passover."

"Why not?"

"We're not Jews."

"We're not Jews here in Capernaum either."

"That's different. Capernaum is full of foreigners and outsiders. Jerusalem, especially during the Passover, is full of Jews - they come from everywhere."

"Ridiculous," Zanah protested. "There'll be so many strangers and foreigners in Jerusalem noone will even notice us."

"You think so?" Rea arched her eyebrows in skepticism.

"Sure. I've heard people come from all over the world, and they're all not there to celebrate the Passover either."

"I don't know. It's at least a three-day journey, maybe four."

"If Jesus can make it, so can we."

"But we're not Jesus. He seems able to go places in no time and without expending any effort."

"His disciples will be going with Him, won't they?"

"I suppose so."

"Then why can't we follow them?" Rea, not completely convinced, agreed and laid back down.

For the next several days, Zanah and Rea watched for signs of Jesus leaving Galilee for Jerusalem. Somehow, they missed seeing Him and His disciples leave, and were not able to go with them as planned. Instead, they attached themselves to a group of pilgrims, vendors and travelers who, upon inquiry, acknowledged they were going to Jerusalem. Noone voiced any objections to Zanah and Rea joining them, it being of no consequence apparently that they were two unattached women and were not Jews. Zanah looked at Rea as if to say, "See, I told you."

****

The most direct route from Capernaum to Jerusalem circled around the Sea of Galilee to the west, bypassing Tiberias and then following the Jordan River. The caravan, numbering perhaps a hundred or more souls, most of them walking and carrying their belongings on their backs - as were Zanah and Rea, though having no belongings to carry - included donkeys, camels, wagons and carts. Zanah observed a few people pulling carts that appeared to be loaded with all they owned - evidently planning for an extended stay. Some herded sheep and goats intended for a sacrificial offering when they reached Jerusalem.

The route would be much shorter, Zanah figured, if they didn't have to follow the river, for it twisted and turned like a giant silvery serpent slithering its way toward its destination. It was impossible to depart from the meandering river and travel straight as a crow flies, for the valley was very narrow - at times not more than a furlong or two wide - mountains rising precipitously on both sides. The mountains shielded the valley from the wind, making traveling hot and exhausting. The caravan crossed over from the west side of the river to the east side, fording the river just below where the Yarmuk River flowed into the Jordan, and just above the village of Bethabara. The driver of the caravan announced they would camp there for the night. There were no dissenters. Everyone, including Zanah and Rea were exhausted.

Fires were built, primarily to ward off wild animals - especially hyenas and jackals. Zanah and Rea, feeling like they belonged, gathered around a fire and listened to others spin yarns and tall tales. Folks shared their food with one another. Noone went hungry. Zanah enjoyed the camaraderie. If anyone was curious about Rea and her, they never made it known. Zanah figured either it never came to their attention, or they didn't care - which was all right with Zanah and Rea.

Zanah awoke the next morning feeling nauseated - which was unusual for her. She was as strong and healthy as a pack mule. The trip from Samaria to

Capernaum hadn't taxed her, why did one day's travel upset her? Perhaps it was something she ate. Managing to conceal her nausea and carry on as usual, she didn't mention it to Rea. As the day wore on, the nausea left her, and she dismissed the matter from her mind.

Zanah noticed a young Jewish man eyeing Rea. When they stopped to rest, he approached Rea and talked to her. His name was Benjamin. He had a small farm outside Chorazin where he lived alone. He said he tried to observe the Passover every year, but admitted missing two or three times. It wasn't convenient leaving the farm in the spring. He asked Rea where she was from and why she was going to Jerusalem, since she had told him she was Syro-Phoenician. Rea was at a loss to provide a logical reason other than telling Benjamin Zanah wanted to go and talked her into going with her. Benjamin didn't ask why Zanah wanted to go. Rea enjoyed the attention, especially since Benjamin didn't fault her for not being Jewish.

Zanah couldn't help noticing Rea and Benjamin were together every opportunity - not that she objected to Rea having a male companion. After all, what right did she have to object? Even so, Rea was her sole companion - the only one she'd had the past three months - and it made her feel alone and left out. She resented Benjamin's intrusion. It was a new and strange experience for her.

Mishtar often went off tending his goats, or wasting away the day with his cronies. He never felt it necessary to confide in Zanah where he was going or what he planned to do; and neither did he concern himself with what she might do while he was gone. Even when he was with her, he often ignored her. Sometimes hours passed without him saying a word. She learned when he was in one of his sullen silent moods, it was useless to complain or try talking to him. The only time he was talkative or paid attention to her was when he wanted something. Still, she never resented it or felt lonely and left out. How or why had she become so dependent on Rea in such a short time?

Through heat waves, like slender strings of silver dancing before her eyes distorting objects on the horizon, Zanah made out the village of Amathus just ahead. Rivulets of perspiration rolled down her face. Dust and dirt clung to her sweaty clothing as if seeking refuge. What she wouldn't give for a good, hot bath where she could just lay there and soak, or even a river where she could strip off her clothes and jump in; but there was no river in Amathus - besides such impropriety was impossible with so many people around. The driver pulled the caravan over to a grove of palm trees and declared a rest period, which Zanah sorely needed. The nausea had weakened her more than she realized. She doubted she could have gone another furlong. Relaxing in the shade, Zanah noted how small Amathus was - not more than ten or eleven mud brick houses. The village seemed out of place here in the desolate valley - like a precious jewel in a pig's snout. Not that Amathus was a precious jewel by any means, but it made her wonder about its reason for being. Except for this grove of date palms, a few citrus trees and a vineyard, there was nothing here. There were no signs of activity, the folks staying inside out of the heat, Zanah presumed. One couldn't blame them.

It was that indecisive period when time can't seem to make up its mind whether to remain daylight or give way to darkness, when the caravan reached the Jabbok River. They forded the stream and made camp. By the time wood had been gathered, fires made and everyone ate, and shared their aches and pains with one another; time had reached a decision and surrendered to total darkness. Finding a grassy spot near one of the fires, Zanah bedded down. She was alone. She had not talked to Rea since morning and, because of Rea's absence, assumed she was spending the night with Benjamin. Zanah had not yet fallen asleep when Rea joined her. Rea offered no explanation or excuse for neglecting Zanah - as if one was needed, or necessary - the reason for the neglect being obvious. Neither did she offer an apology.

All Rea wanted to talk about was Benjamin, and it was beginning to irritate Zanah. She'd had enough of Benjamin. Why did Rea agree to go to Jerusalem if all she wanted was a man? There were plenty of them in Capernaum. Apparently Rea didn't feel as strongly about Jesus as she did; in spite of the fact Jesus had freed her from her demons. Rea's lifestyle in Capernaum was proof of that; and now she had found a man before the first day's journey was over. Zanah speculated Rea could find a man even in a harem. She remembered Jesus saying something about when an evil spirit comes out of a person, it seeks a place to rest, but can't find any. So it returns to the person it left, and finds the house swept clean. Then it takes seven other spirits more wicked than itself to live there, and the condition of the person is worse than before. Is that the way it is with Rea? Rea would forget Jesus in a minute for Benjamin, or some other man. Well, that was Rea's problem; she had problems of her own.

Rea finally stopped talking about Benjamin and went to sleep. Zanah hoped she didn't talk in her sleep because surely it would be about Benjamin. Zanah pondered her own life. Looking up into the ebony void that seemed to extend into infinity, she tried locating Orion, Pegasus, Sagitarius - vaguely remembering when she was a little girl, someone pointing them out to her - and wondered if Nicholas was looking at these same stars, and thinking of her. She could almost feel his strong arms around her, as if their love transcended time and space. At this moment, her desire for Nicholas far exceeded her desire for Jesus. It surprised her. She hadn't thought about Jesus all day. Recalling her criticism of Rea for the exact same thing, she felt guilty - but only for a moment. She fell asleep.

****

Zanah awoke the third morning again feeling nauseated. Her nausea was more pronounced and of longer duration than the previous day, so that she was unable to conceal it from Rea, nor did she try.

"Zanah, what' s wrong with you?"

Clutching her stomach and gasping for breath, Zanah spoke between spells of vomiting. "I, —I don't know. This is the second morning I' ve been sick."

"Second morning? Zanah, are you pregnant?"

"I can't be, I mean, —no, - I, I don't know."

The possibility she was pregnant upset her. Yes, she had been with Nicholas that night. Was she pregnant with his child? It was more than she could comprehend. How could she be pregnant? Five husbands and Mishtar, and she never got pregnant. She had assumed she couldn't have children. And now, one night with Nicholas, and she's with child? Zanah was not happy about the prospect - not that she didn't want Nicholas' child, but not now. Perhaps she wasn't pregnant, just sick. It was too early to be certain. Pulling herself together, she said, "I'll be all right in a little while. It will pass."

"Are you sure? Can I get you something?"

"No. No, just let me rest."

When the caravan was ready to move out, Zanah had recovered sufficiently to continue. After fording the Jordan, they were back on the west side of the river again heading south toward Jericho. Fortunately for Zanah, those pulling carts and herding sheep and goats kept the pace slow. As the day wore on, she felt better, regaining her strength and the nausea easing. By the time they reached the village of Phasaelis, she was feeling no nausea at all.

Phasaelis, Zanah learned, was laid out by Herod the Great and named after his brother, Phasael. Why did Herod name such a small, obscure village after his brother? Was it his way of telling Phasael he was small and insignificant, Zanah wondered? It seemed to her if Herod really loved his brother, he would've named a city, or at the very least a library, after him. Except that it was on the trade route to Jericho and hence to Jerusalem, like so many small villages they had encountered, she saw no reason for Phasaelis to exist either. Maybe Herod thought when he founded Phasaelis, it would become important. But then, as small and insignificant as she was, what reason did she have to exist? Would she ever be important? She guessed she was to Nicholas - especially now that she was carrying his child. Rea was spending more and more time with Benjamin, only checking on occasion to see if Zanah was all right. During rest stops, Rea rested with Benjamin. Zanah guessed you could call it resting. They were always off in a huddle by themselves. Zanah tried ignoring it and sloughing it off, but it wasn't easy. The only time she and Rea talked was at night, and Zanah assumed that was only because Benjamin didn't want to start a scandal and stir up trouble by letting her sleep with him.

Alone and left out, feeling the need for someone to talk to, Zanah eyed the driver of the caravan. He looked like an amiable, agreeable sort of man, sporting a sly grin and a mischievous twinkle in his eyes - as if he was about to tell a joke, or play a trick. He reminded Zanah of Mishtar, not in manner but appearance - short, stocky, black graying hair and short beard. Fittingly enough, his name was Moses. Sidling up to him, Zanah engaged him in conversation.

"My name is Zanah. Mind if I walk with you?"

"Suit yourself." His voice was warm and inviting.

"Where are you from?"

"Nazareth," Moses replied. "Born and raised there."

"Do you drive caravans all the time?"

"No, just when I'm going to the Passover."

"What do you do the rest of the time?"

"You ask a lot of questions. I thought you just wanted to walk with me." He grinned good-naturedly.

"I'm sorry. I didn't mean to be so inquisitive. It's just that I don't have anyone to talk to."

"What about your friend?"

"Rea? She's taken up with Benjamin."

"So I've noticed. You don't have anyone?"

Shaking her head negatively, Zanah replied, "My man's in Alexandria."

"Alexandria! That's a long ways away."

"He's a trader. He travels all over."

"I see. How's it happen you aren' t with him?"

"We're not married yet. I'm going to join him later." She paused for a moment. "You said you were from Nazareth. You must know Jesus."

"Known Him all His life."

"What was He like - as a boy, I mean?"

"Like any boy."

"Do you think He's the Messiah?"

"Nope."

"Why not?"

"Why not!?" Moses looked at her, astonished. "Look at Him! Wanders all over the country. No job, no property, no money, no responsibility - and He's going to deliver Israel from her enemies?"

"I'm sorry. I didn't mean to upset you, but what about all the miracles?"

"Tricks. Magic. Illusions," Moses sniffed. "Do you think He's the Messiah?"

"I don't know. He says He is."

"That don't mean He is."

"No, I suppose not."

"You're Samaritan, aren't you." Zanah noted it was a statement, not a question.

Frustrated, not knowing whether to admit it or deny it, Zanah felt humbled. "Yes," she muttered. She hoped her admission wouldn't change anything. She liked Moses in spite of his opinion of Jesus. He was company, which she definitely needed.

"I thought so. I could tell from your accent. Aren't you taking a chance going to Jerusalem? You know how most Jews feel about Samaritans."

Relieved Moses had said, "Most Jews," Zanah took that to mean he didn't share their prejudice. "Yes, I know," she said.

"Then why are you going?"

"It's kind of hard to explain. All I can say is I met Jesus once in Samaria, and ever since then I've had this desire to know Him. My life changed. I don't know if He had anything to do with that, but I have to find out."

They came to Archelais, a village founded and named by Herod Archelaus, ethnarch of Judaea many years ago. Moses told Zanah Archelaus was banished to Vienna in Gaul by Caesar Augustus. Moses decided to halt the caravan for a rest and inspection. Leaving Zanah, he went throughout the caravan, checking to see if all was well.

While Moses was making his inspection, Zanah sat on a rock rubbing her aching feet and resting her weary body. No reason to seek out Rea. Reflecting on what Moses had told her about Archelaus, she concluded the village had fared better than its founder. It looked quite prosperous - which was more than she could say for the other villages they had passed through. From her vantage point outside the village, she could see innumerable limestone houses and buildings - several of them quite large. There was considerable activity within the village - far more than in the other villages.

Finding no problems, Moses returned to Zanah. The journey had been surprisingly trouble-free so far, considering the number of wagons, carts and animals in the caravan.

"Everything all right?" Zanah asked.

"Everything's fine," Moses replied. For several minutes they were both silent. Moses broke the silence. "Where are you staying in Jerusalem?"

"I don't know. We," hopefully including Rea, "don't have a place."

"You won't find any rooms available during Passover week. They are all taken."

"Then we'll sleep in a stable or on the ground. I've done it before."

"1 don't recommend it. It's not like any other time. Jerusalem will be crowded. Every kind of human being imaginable, besides religious folks and pilgrims, will be there - merchants, traders, hustlers, loan sharks, thieves, murderers, rapists. You name it, they'll be there looking for a quick farthing or an easy victim."

"I heard Pilate sends extra legionnaires to control the crowd during Passover."

"Humph!" Moses sniffed. "They're no better than the others." Knowing Antonio, Zanah understood what Moses meant.

"What can we do?"

"I hate to see a young woman like you get into trouble. I have a friend in Jerusalem named Simeon - he's a potter - who might be willing to put you up."

"Do you think he would?" Zanah beamed with excitement.

"When we get to Jerusalem, I' ll take you to him. If he can, I'm sure he will help you."

"Oh, thank you." Zanah hugged Moses' neck, causing him to sputter with embarrassment.

"Time to move out," Moses said, getting up. "Let's move!" he shouted.

There was much scurrying as everyone scrambled to their feet, gathered up their belongings and strapped them on their backs. The squeaking of wheels was heard again as camels and donkeys kicked up clouds of dust. Moses had told the people that, short of an emergency, they would not stop again until they reached Jericho, seven and a half miles to the south.

Zanah continued walking alongside Moses. They talked about things in general - weather, crops, government. She was careful not to broach the subject of the Messiah, or Jesus. Moses had turned out to be a good friend, and she didn't want to tax their relationship.

Convinced she was pregnant, the initial shock having worn off, Zanah not only accepted it, but was elated. She would've preferred it happen at a more convenient time, but she couldn't think of anything that would give her more pleasure than to present Nicholas with a son - it just had to be a boy. She tried imagining what it would be like having a child to raise. How would Nicholas receive the news? She hadn't considered that. What if he didn't want children - he traveled and was gone so much. What then? What if he didn't believe the child was his? After all, Nicholas was well aware of her clouded past. What assurance did he have she had remained faithful? She began to tremble.

Trying to regain her composure and jubilation, she reasoned a man as kind, honest and gentle as Nicholas would surely want a family, especially a son. She believed that, in spite of her past, Nicholas trusted her, and she wasn't about to betray that trust. What kind of life would they have if they couldn't trust each other? She was proud to be carrying Nicholas' child. At the first opportunity, she would send him a note telling him the news.

Only a gold and red glow in the west was all that remained of the bright sunlight when Jericho loomed on the horizon. Zanah's heart leaped with wild anticipation. To think, she was going to visit Jericho. Never in her wildest dreams did she ever picture herself walking through the streets of Jericho - or the streets of Jerusalem, for that matter. Recalling her conversation with Jesus at the well, she had said, "You Jews say Jerusalem is the place to worship." Jesus had replied, "The time is coming when you will worship in neither Jerusalem or Mount Gerizim, but in spirit and truth." Well, she had the right spirit, didn't she, and wasn't she seeking the truth? If she didn't have the right spirit, she never would have left Samaria, let alone attempt to go to Jerusalem during Passover Week - or was it foolhardiness? Anyway, she was nearing Jericho.

Approaching the walled city, Zanah became aware theirs was not the only caravan converging on Jericho. On the trail, they had not seen any others, but now she saw caravans, some of them much larger than theirs, as well as a multitude of individuals traveling on their own, all coming together from every direction. Moses said it would be impossible to drive a caravan through the narrow, crowded streets. They would circle the city and make camp on the south side. Remembering how congested Samaria and Capernaum were - Jericho would be much worse - Zanah knew Moses was right, but she was disappointed just the same. She noticed other caravans were doing the same thing.

On the south side of Jericho, chaos of the highest disorder reigned with everyone fighting for an unoccupied space on which to make camp. Zanah wished they would settle down. The clamor and din was giving her a headache. She held her cloak over her nose and mouth in order to breathe, the wagons and animals keeping the dust stirred up. She marveled at Moses' competence. This was where he earned his pay, she supposed. Out on the open road, there wasn't much to do. The small villages they passed through presented no difficulties; but keeping the caravan together and finding a suitable campsite in this bedlam, was a monumental task - to which Moses proved capable. After arguing and drawing in the dirt with several of the other drivers, Moses staked out a claim, and everyone bedded down.

Zanah was surprised when Rea showed up. She was excited as she told Rea about Moses' friend who might provide them a place to stay.

"I'm not going with you," Rea stated. The blood drained from Zanah's face as if she had been stabbed with a knife.

"Not going? Why not? I thought we, —us…"

"Benjamin has asked me to stay with him. He wants me to go with him to Chorazin after the Passover."

"I see," Zanah said, turning away from Rea to hide the pain written on her face.

Zanah was scared. Just like that, Rea terminated their relationship, as if it was nothing more than a passing fancy. Until now, Zanah only felt alone, but now the realization hit her; she was alone. She felt maligned, deserted. There was strength in two. There was courage in two. There was safety in two. With Rea, Zanah wasn't afraid to attempt anything. But alone? It was as if the wind had been let out of her sails, and she was cast adrift, left to the mercy of the winds and currents of the world.

Zanah held Rea with contempt. Everything was going so well. She and Rea got along beautifully, and then she let Benjamin ruin everything. How could she? And then it occurred to Zanah, what if it had been the other way around? Suppose Rea had walked out on Benjamin and stayed with her; and then after she had completed her quest, she said to Rea, "I've found what I was seeking, so now I'm leaving you and going to my man in Alexandria." Then Rea would be the one maligned, deserted. Rea would feel the pain she was feeling.

No, Zanah had no right to fault Rea or Benjamin. If Rea has found what she wants, who can blame her for claiming it? There was no turning back now. She had gone beyond the point of no return. "Accept what you can't change, screw up your courage and continue your quest," she told herself. "You aren't completely alone; there's Moses."

"I' II miss you, Rea," Zanah said, brushing the tears from her eyes. "You've been a good friend. I hope you and Benjamin will be happy."

"Thank you. You too. I hope you find what you' re looking for." They hugged one another, and Rea departed.

Zanah never saw Rea again. She knew Rea was with Benjamin somewhere in the caravan, but didn't try to search her out. She took her place alongside Moses.

****

Zanah reckoned it would be impossible for anyone on the highway not to go to Jerusalem. The tide of people would sweep them along like a log caught in a rampaging river. They would be swept on to Jerusalem whether they wanted to go there or not. What would a traveler do if he wanted to go in the opposite direction? Zanah guessed he would just have to abandon the idea. The going became more arduous, for the elevation rose sharply from Jericho to Jerusalem. Zanah presumed some in the caravan had not anticipated the steep grades - especially those pulling wagons and carts; for she saw them being abandoned, and their owners taking with them only what belongings they could carry. Those already carrying their possessions discarded some of their belongings to lighten their load. Zanah retrieved some of the things for herself. Some of the older more feeble fell by the wayside. Few seemed to care, or stopped to render aid. How terrible! How uncharitable, Zanah thought. Everyone seemed bent on one thing - getting to Jerusalem whatever the cost. Zanah appreciated being young and healthy. Even so, the climb took all the strength and stamina she could muster. Her pregnancy didn't hinder her walking, and she hadn't experienced any more nausea. Although it was not yet the sixth hour, Zanah felt as if she was walking through hades itself. Through sweat-blurred eyes, she beheld Bethany, an obscure little village less than an hour's walk from Jerusalem. Her heart beat faster with every step taking her closer to Jerusalem, forgetting at least for the time being, the uncertainties she faced alone. Passing the Mount of Olives, just west of the city, she looked down on the great walled city spread out before her.

Jerusalem sat on a flat plateau surrounded on three sides by deep valleys with precipitous sides, giving it the appearance of a fortress. The highway ran virtually parallel to the valley of the Kidron on the eastern side of the city. Olive trees dotted the countryside. Otherwise the land was rocky with only small patches of grass here and there. Crossing over a bridge spanning the valley, they went north for a short distance before stopping at a gate to the city.

Before entering the city, Moses moved the caravan to an open area. Thanking everyone for making the trip pleasant and trouble-free, he announced this was as far as he was escorting them. From here on, each party was on their own, responsible for their own welfare and well-being. He turned to Zanah and said, "You, come with me."

Taking up the few belongings she had accumulated, Zanah went with Moses - glad to be with him, for the strange surroundings and great number of people were overwhelming. She never envisioned such chaos. A person can get themselves in a lot of trouble through ignorance and impetuousness, she mused alluding to her own, and the trouble she would be in were it not for Moses. Her own astuteness made her smile. The surging crowd swept Moses and her through the gate. Fearful of getting separated from Moses, she was careful to stay close to him - not knowing where Simeon lived or how to get there.

They passed a great stone wall with five archways leading to a pool. Moses said this was Bethesda, meaning "the flowing water." He told her it was the only natural spring in Jerusalem. It had once been outside the city, but Herod the Great extended the wall to include Bethesda. Zanah was impressed with Moses' knowledge of history.

Their course took them past a massive stone building Zanah said resembled a fortress. Moses told her it was, indeed, a fortress - the Fortress of Antonia. The name rekindled unpleasant memories of Antonio. Zanah hoped she didn't encounter him again, especially since she didn't have Leukas or Nicholas to defend her. She wasn't sure how much help Moses would be. Pilate stayed at the fortress whenever he was in Jerusalem, and he made it a point to be in Jerusalem during Passover Week - or any other Jewish celebration - to forestall any potential rioting by the Jews. Noticing the presence of a number of legionnaires, Moses informed her the building also housed the palace guard. Another gate led to a large open area - that is, it would have been open were it not overrun with people, cluttered with stalls, tents and booths offering everything from dried fish and goat meat to rugs and carpets. The stench emanating from the fish and meat stalls caused Zanah's nausea to return. She hurried past them. The aroma from the booths selling spices and incense was much more appealing.

Zanah had little opportunity to look at all that was for sale or inspect the quality of the merchandise from being pushed and shoved by the throng. It was just as well - she couldn't buy anything anyway. The entire area was a sea of pandemonium. People were shouting, haggling over prices or complaining about the merchandise, often boisterous for no apparent reason. Zanah concluded it was a way of life for the Jews. They thrived on it. Life wouldn't be nearly as enjoyable if they couldn't argue and barter.

Moses stopped at a shop displaying pottery of every size, shape and description. Zanah saw a thin, slight-built, stoop-shouldered man working the pottery wheel. This must be Simeon, she thought. He looked to be about the same age as Moses, although not as hairy. His head was as bald as an ostrich egg except for a fringe of salt and pepper hair continuing into a flowing beard. Heavy gray eyebrows hovered over a pair of brown eyes and an overly large nose. Fascinated,

Zanah watched as his wet, soiled hands deftly worked the clay. Simeon did not see them enter.

"Simeon," Moses said.

"Moses, old friend," Simeon said, stopping the wheel. "Good to see you again." He wiped the grime off his hands, and extended his hand to Moses. "You haven't changed a bit since last year."

"Neither have you, you old buzzard." Moses shook Simeon's hand, and they hugged each other. Simeon looked puzzled when his eyes fell on Zanah.

"This is Zanah," Moses said, taking note of Simeon's curious expression. "A friend of mine."

Simeon studied Zanah for a moment and then looked at Moses.

"Moses, you old rascal."

"Now wait," Moses protested. "It's not what you're thinking. Zanah and her friend were in my caravan, and her friend deserted her. She doesn't know anyone in Jerusalem, or have a place to stay. I told her you might be able to help her." Moses saw the look of doubt on Simeon's face. "Honest, Simeon, that's all there is to it." Zanah had to smile at Simeon's insinuation.

"Any friend of Moses' is a friend of mine. Welcome." He offered his hand to Zanah.

"Thank you, Sir," Zanah said, accepting Simeon's hand.

"You must both be worn out. Come, everything's ready for you. Martha will be delighted to see you."

The mention of Martha made Zanah feel uneasy. She hadn't known what to expect. Moses had said only that he had a friend who might help her. She assumed Moses would drop her off at Simeon's, and Simeon would find her a place to stay - perhaps at an inn. It never occurred to her Simeon would be married, and she would be staying in a private home with Moses. How would Simeon's wife receive her, a stranger and a Samaritan? It didn't appear to disturb Simeon. Surely he noticed she wasn't a Jewess. Would his wife - what was her name, Martha - be as gracious? The question put butterflies in her stomach.

A door at the rear of the pottery shed led into a walled courtyard with a well in the center. Zanah speculated how much she would've enjoyed the convenience of having a well at her doorstep in Sychar. Then she wouldn't have had to go to Jacob's well and put up with Gabah. A stone, flat-roof house fitted into one corner of the courtyard. It was larger and nicer than most houses Zanah had ever seen. A wood ladder gave access to the roof. There were four date palms alongside the house.

Throughout the courtyard lilies, roses and anemone bloomed. A bed of herbs and spices emitted a pungent, but pleasant, aroma. Zanah guessed Simeon did quite well with his business to afford such as this.

Entering through a door into the inner court, a large sunlit room lighted by a skylight that could be covered in the event of inclement weather, greeted them. Immediately to the right was a room where, Zanah was told, she would sleep. Directly opposite on the other side of the court was a similar room, which was assigned to Moses. Simeon's and Martha's room adjoined Moses' room. Entrance was gained through a doorway off the court. On the other side of the court, an opening led to the dining area. The kitchen was behind the rear wall of the court, accessible from either Simeon's room or the dining area.

"Martha, Moses is here!" Simeon called out. A tall slender woman, nearly a head taller than Simeon - who Zanah guessed to be about five foot seven - emerged from the kitchen by way of the dining area. Zanah noted Martha was fairer than most Jewish women - causing her to wonder if Martha might be of some other descent. Light brown hair done up in a bun, blue eyes, slender nose and thin lips strengthened her assumption Martha wasn't a Jew. Was that why Moses didn't hesitate to invite her into their home?

"How good to see you again," Martha said, taking Moses' hand. She glanced at Zanah as if to say, "And who is this?"

"This is Zanah, my friend. Now don't go jumping to conclusions like Simeon did. She's strictly a friend."

"Welcome, dear," Martha said, extending her hand to Zanah." I hope you will feel at home."

"Thank you." Zanah accepted Martha's hand. There was nothing inhospitable about Martha's manner - easing Zanah's tension.

"You can put your things in that room, Moses," Martha said, indicating the room on their left. "And, Zanah, you may put your things in this room," indicating the room on the right. "There's water in the pitcher. You can freshen up a bit, and then we'll eat."

Zanah took her things into the room. It wasn't a large room, nor was it lavishly furnished, but the furnishings were adequate and of good quality - much better than anything she was accustomed to. The room included a bed, chair and washstand with a clay basin, pitcher and water jar - no doubt made by Simeon's own hands. Several pegs on the wall were for hanging clothes. A bracket on another wall held an oil lamp. The tile floor was partially covered with reed mats. Zanah wondered if Simeon also made the floor tiles. Most houses she had been in had dirt floors. A small, square opening in the front wall looked out onto the courtyard and admitted the day's last rays of light. Splashing water on her face and washing her hands, Zanah reflected on her good fortune. She had thought Rea and her would tour Jerusalem together, making out as best they could - sleeping on the ground or in some stable, and eating whatever someone gave them. She realized now, they never would have survived. But because of Moses' charity, she was with friends and living in the lap of luxury - at least what was luxury to her. Why did Moses befriend her? Was he simply a kind-hearted man, or did he fathom the danger she was subjecting herself to? She remembered him saying, "I hate to see a young woman like you get into trouble." Whatever his motive, he saved her from certain disaster, and she owed him a debt of gratitude.

Martha and Simeon graciously accepted her on the strength of Moses' word, "She's a friend." No questions asked. Zanah couldn't help noticing, every time she faced a crisis lately, someone always came to her aid. It was as if she was living a charmed life. The mystery continued to recur in her mind. Drying herself on a towel, she joined the others in the dining area.

The dining room contained a long, heavy, wood table with long benches on both sides. That was all the furniture in the room. There were no windows. A wood cross with an oil lamp affixed to the end of each arm was suspended from the ceiling, furnishing light.

Simeon and Moses sat on one side of the table, conversing about events from the year past and political issues. Martha and Zanah sat on the other side of the table.

"How did you meet Moses, my dear?" Martha asked.

"A friend and I joined his caravan in Capernaum."

"Are you from Capernaum?"

"No, I'm from Sychar in Samaria."

"Then you are a Samaritan?"

"Yes." Zanah held her breath, the muscles in her face tightening, as she awaited Martha's reply.

"You know the Jews hate the Samaritans." Zanah noted it was not an inquiry, but a statement of fact.

"Yes, I know." She was getting tired of hearing the same thing all the time. It irritated her. She steeled herself against Martha's retort.

"Then why, may I ask, have you come to Jerusalem?"

"I knew Jesus would be here, and I wanted to see Him." The mention of Jesus didn't offend Moses, Zanah recalled, but how would Martha react? Zanah assumed Moses never would have brought her here if either Simeon or Martha would be offended - but it was only an assumption. There being no way to avoid the issue or change the subject, Zanah decided to be honest and straight-forward, letting happen whatever would.

"Do you think Jesus is the Messiah?" Martha's voice was soft and kind, not harsh or abrasive.

"I don't know. That's what I hope to find out."

"I see." Martha paused, as if weighing her words. "Simeon and I have talked about Him."

"What did you decide?" She began to relax.

"We both agreed, He couldn't be the Messiah."

"Why not?"

"Well, for one thing, nearly all His followers are poor people, common people. Not that there's anything wrong with being poor," Martha added, realizing Zanah was about as poor and common as they come. "But you can't build a kingdom with poor people. You have to have followers who are rich, powerful, influential."

"I guess you' re right; but just the same, I want to find out for myself - for my own satisfaction."

"How do you propose doing that?"

Zanah inhaled and let out a deep breath. Why does everyone think I have to have some specific plan? She was as tired of hearing that as she was the Jews hated the Samaritans. Managing to conceal her exasperation - she hoped - she replied. "I don't have a plan. I'll just find Jesus, and see what happens."

"I understand He doesn't stay in Jerusalem, but stays with friends in Bethany. You might begin your search there. Bethany is just a short walk from here. You passed through it just before you got to Jerusalem."

"Yes, I remember it." Zanah wondered why Martha offered this bit of information. Why was she willing to help - especially since she and Simeon didn't believe Jesus is the Messiah? Although Martha never intimated she was anything but Jewish, Zanah now felt certain she wasn't. Perhaps she was a proselyte, having been converted to Judaism. Not being a Jew might explain her willingness to help. Whatever the reason, Zanah welcomed the information and thanked her.

It was still the first watch when Zanah, saying she wanted to get an early start in the morning, excused herself and retired to her room. Reflecting on her conversation with Martha, Zanah pondered the reasons everyone gave for not believing Jesus was the Messiah. Leukas thought Jesus was a con artist. Moses thought Jesus was too irresponsible - a drifter. Martha thought He lacked powerful, influential followers. Even Rea, who was a recipient of Jesus' healing couldn't be thought of as a true believer - giving up her pursuit for the arms of a man. At least she didn't let Nicholas dissuade her. None of them gave any credence to the miracles He performed.

Everyone said people followed Jesus out of curiosity, or for what He could do for them. Doubt clouded Zanah's mind. Why was she following Him? Wasn't it curiosity? She couldn't say she believed in Him. What did she want Him to do for her? Was she looking for some miracle - like being healed? No. Yes, she was curious, but it was more than idle curiosity that was driving her on. It was more like an inner compulsion. She couldn't help herself. She had to resolve the question to her own satisfaction - is He or isn't He the Messiah? In the morning she would go to Bethany.

****

Zanah was up with the sun. To her surprise, Martha was already up and about. Even more surprising, Martha had fixed a lunch for Zanah to take along, telling her she might get hungry before the day was over. Accepting the lunch, Zanah thanked her.

"Do you think you can find your way?" Martha asked.

"I think so."

"Just go back the way you came, and it will take you to Bethany. You may leave your things here."

"Thank you. You' re very kind."

"Be careful. Don't get involved with strangers. There are a lot of unsavory characters here during Passover Week."

"I'll be careful."

Walking through the courtyard and Simeon's pottery shed, Zanah emerged onto the street, already teeming with people - peddlers, traders and shopkeepers already doing a brisk business. Pushing and shoving her way through the throng, Zanah easily found the gate through which she and Moses had passed the day before. Turning east, she passed the Fortress of Antonia. Before she reached the pool of Bethesda, Zanah saw a host of people approaching - shouting and waving palm branches. As they drew nearer, Zanah saw they were going before a man astride a donkey. They laid palm branches in his path. Some even took off their outer cloak and laid it in His path. They were shouting, "Hosanna! Hosanna on the highest! Hosanna to the son of David! Blessed is He who comes in the name of the Lord!" Drawing even closer, she saw the man on the donkey was Jesus. She followed the procession, and got caught up in the spirit of the throng.

The procession moved past the pool of Bethesda and the Fortress of Antonia, Zanah jubilantly celebrating with the others. Pilgrims, merchants and religious leaders taking notice of the celebration and the man on the donkey, looked at one another in astonishment wondering, "Who is this?" Winding through the streets, past the shops and booths, the procession crossed over the Tyropeon Valley to the outer court of the temple. Many brought their blind and lame to be healed. Zanah watched in awe and fascination as Jesus healed them all. As the hour grew late, Jesus and His disciples left Jerusalem for the night; returning to Bethany Zanah presumed.

Certain Jesus would return the next day, Zanah decided not to follow Him to Bethany. Instead, full of stories and excitement, she hurried to Simeon's house. If Martha was surprised to see her, she never let on. Zanah, bubbling over, described to Simeon, Martha and Moses the procession - people shouting "Hosanna," Jesus healing the blind and lame at the temple. She was disappointed. None of them shared her enthusiasm, but neither did they try to dampen her spirit. Sleep was impossible. She was wound up and tight as a bowstring. Thursday Zanah returned to the temple courtyard just as she had Tuesday and

Wednesday; but Jesus and His disciples weren't there. She paced back and forth all day, waiting for Him; but He never appeared. Did the rulers of the temple make good their threat to kill Him, she wondered? She questioned some women who were gathered there at the temple. Did they know where Jesus was? One woman told her Jesus and His disciples were shut up in a room where they were observing the Passover supper. She told Zanah where the house was, and Zanah went there - watching and waiting outside.

Night fell. Shivering, Zanah wrapped her cloak around her - it felt clammy, providing no warmth. The cobblestone streets glistened with dew, and the marble bench was wet and cold. Endeavoring to keep warm, she huddled in the doorway of an adjacent building and fell asleep.

Zanah didn't know how long she had been asleep, when the clamor and din of a procession of men bearing torches aroused her. Through the mist she saw some of the men, armed with clubs and swords, escorting a man toward the temple. Curious as to what was taking place, she followed the procession. She saw the man being escorted was Jesus, and He was bound. What had He done to stir up such a ruckus in the middle of the night? What were they going to do with Him?

Zanah followed as the men took Jesus to Caiaphas, the high priest, and the council chamber of the Sanhedrin on the south edge of the outer court of the temple. She waited outside with the others.

"What are they doing with Jesus?" Zanah asked a bystander.

"They're holding His trial."

"Trial? In the middle of the night? What has He done?"

"What has He done! Woman, where have you been these past days? He's blasphemed God! Claimed to be God! Said He's a king! Threatened to destroy this temple! And you ask what has He done!? I hope they kill Him!" Zanah knew better than to say anything further.

The hours dragged on. Zanah forgot about being cold. The crowd was growing restless, and becoming more raucous and angry as the night wore on. Rumors and accusations spread like a plague, stirring the crowd to the brink of rebellion. Zanah feared, not only for Jesus, but for her own life. Someone built a fire in the courtyard, for the cold and dampness was escalating the mob's impatience. Zanah saw one of Jesus' disciples standing by the fire warming himself. It was the big one, the one Rea said was Peter. At least here was someone she dared speak to.

"You also were with Jesus in Galilee," Zanah said.

"I don't know what you're talking about. I don't know the man." Peter spoke loud enough for everyone to hear, and then walked away, mingling with the crowd.

Zanah thought it strange for Peter to deny knowing Jesus. Could she have been mistaken? No, there was no mistaking him - it was Peter. She wasn't accusing him of anything. She just wanted someone she could talk to. Evidently that was the problem, she decided. The mob was angry at Jesus. They wanted to kill Him. If they knew Peter was one of His disciples, they would want to kill him too. She could relate to that. Only a short time ago she had refused to speak up in favor of Jesus herself. To have done so would've provoked the man's wrath; so she had said nothing. Peter was doing the same thing, and she didn't blame him.

At daybreak, the high priest and members of the council emerged with Jesus still in their custody. Caiaphas announced to the frenzied crowd, they had found Jesus guilty of blasphemy, inciting a riot and insurrection, sentencing Him to death. The court did not have the authority to carry out a death sentence, Caiaphas informed them; so they were taking Him to Pilate, the Roman Procurator. Zanah followed, as they led Jesus, still bound, to the Fortress of Antonia and Pilate's court. Pilate, seated on the judgment seat on the porch of the palace, met with the mob.

"We have found this man guilty of subverting our nation," the spokesman for the council stated. "He opposes paying taxes to Caesar, and claims to be Christ, a king."

"Are you king of the Jews?" Pilate asked.

"Yes, it is as you say," Jesus said, causing an uproar and stirring among the crowd.

"I find no basis for a charge against this man," Pilate said.

"He stirs up the people all over Judaea," the spokesman insisted. "He started in Galilee, and has come all the way, here."

"Are you a Galilean?" Pilate asked. Jesus acknowledged He was. "This man is under Herod's jurisdiction. Take him to Herod," Pilate ordered, and immediately retreated to inside the palace.

Zanah followed the angry mob as they led Jesus to Herod's palace. Herod was greatly pleased to see Jesus because for a long time he had been wanting to meet Him. He heard about the miracles Jesus performed, and hoped to see Jesus perform some miracle. For considerable time, Herod plied Jesus with questions, but Jesus refused to answer him.

Zanah wondered why Jesus remained silent. Why didn't He offer an explanation? Why didn't He say something in His own defense? She heard the chief priest and the teachers of the law vehemently accuse Jesus. Herod ordered the soldiers to take Jesus, dress Him in a purple robe and put a crown of thorns on His head. The mob mocked and ridiculed Jesus, and spat on Him. Zanah threw her hands over her mouth and gasped as the blood streamed down Jesus' face from the crown of thorns jammed on His head. Feeling faint, she diverted her eyes from the scene. Why didn't He do something? Silently she urged Jesus to resist - although she knew it would be ineffectual. To her dismay, Jesus took the abuse and humiliation without so much as lifting His hand or uttering a cry; and then Herod told the high priest and rabbis to take Him back to Pilate.

Pilate summoned the high priest, the rulers of the synagogue and the teachers of the law, and said to them, "You brought me this man as one who was inciting the people to rebellion. I have examined Him in your presence and have found no basis for your charges against Him. Neither has Herod, for he sent Him back to us. As you can see, He has done nothing to deserve death. Therefore, I will punish Him and release Him."

The mob was outraged. They had been coached what to say by the chief priest and the council. With one voice they cried out, "Away with this man! Release Barabbas!" Barabbas was in prison for murder and insurrection. Pilate wanted to release Jesus, Zanah believed, and she hoped he would; but the mob kept shouting, "Crucify Him! Crucify Him!"

"Why?" Pilate asked. "What crime has He committed?" The crowd, becoming increasingly rebellious, demanded Jesus be crucified. Not wanting to provoke a riot, Pilate gave in to their demand and released Barabbas to them. Zanah stifled a cry. She wanted to cry out, "No," but she knew the rebellious crowd would turn on her. They were out for blood. Pilate was releasing a murderer and punishing an innocent man. He ordered Jesus scourged.

Stripping Jesus of His cloak, the soldiers laid the whip to His back. The sharp metal tips on the leather thongs dug into Jesus' back, tearing out chunks of flesh and sending rivers of blood coursing down His back. Jesus' knees buckled with each lash of the whip. Again and again the whip was laid across His back, each time making new, deeper wounds, sending more blood flowing. Unable to stomach the gruesome sight,

Zanah turned her eyes away; but she could still hear the crack of the whip, and cringed each time. When at last the scourging stopped, she saw Jesus on His knees, half dead from the scourging and loss of blood.

Pilate ordered Jesus to take up His cross and carry it outside the city where He was to be crucified. Jesus stumbled under the weight of the cross, and Pilate ordered a man from Cyrene standing nearby, to carry the cross for Him. Sick to her stomach and, although not desiring to witness anymore bloodshed and brutality, Zanah followed the procession out the gate and up the hill called Mount Calvary, as if propelled by some mysterious outside force. She watched the soldiers pound the large spikes through Jesus' hands and feet, pinning Him to the cross - vomiting with each blow of the hammer until there was nothing left in her to throw up. The soldiers raised the cross and dropped it into the hole with a sickening thud. She couldn't take any more. In a state of shock, her senses numbed, she turned away, stumbling down the hill and staggering in the direction of the city.

Confused and disoriented, Zanah wandered without any aim or purpose; unmindful of her surroundings or anybody. Bumping into someone, she felt them grip her arm hard until it ached. "Well, well, look who's here." Zanah didn't need to see the face to know who it was had a death-grip on her arm. She recognized the voice as that of Antonio. He dragged her toward a passageway. She struggled to free herself, but he was too strong. "There's nobody here to protect you now," he sneered. Suddenly there was total darkness even though it was midday. Zanah was startled, as was Antonio; causing him to momentarily loosen his grip on Zanah's arm. Taking advantage of Antonio's lapse, she jerked free and ran as fast as she could in the dark; frequently bumping into and stumbling over objects and falling - expecting Antonio to pounce on her each time. The sudden darkness baffled her, but she didn't have time to think about that. She had to get as far away from Antonio as possible. Not daring to slow down or look back, she kept running without any sense of direction or destination until she fell to the ground exhausted. Believing Antonio was right on her heels, she waited with trepidation for him to assault her. Nothing happened. Had she lost him? Getting up off the ground, she staggered to a nearby doorway, hoping to hide and catch her breath. The sudden darkness, what caused it? Was the world coming to an end? In light of Antonio and all that had happened to Jesus, she didn't care if it did.

About the ninth hour, the darkness gave way to bright daylight as suddenly and mysteriously as it had come. People quickly gathered in small groups debating, with much spirit, the crucifixion and the sudden darkness. Zanah heard some say the darkness fell at the exact same hour Jesus died. "Truly He was God," they said. Others ridiculed the notion, saying it was mere coincidence. Everyone seemed to have an opinion or explanation except Zanah. She was just relieved the darkness was gone, and so was Antonio. It was daylight, as it should be. But Jesus was gone too, and that was not as it should be. Calling to mind the crucifixion, her nausea returned.

In eluding Antonio, Zanah had lost all sense of direction, and had no concept as to where she was.

Thousands of people were milling around, but conscious of her Samaritan origin, and not wanting to invite trouble, she was afraid to ask anyone for directions. Besides, as despondent as she was, where she was didn't matter anyway. When Jesus died, her aspiration died as well. Her whole objective had been singular - know more about Jesus. Now there was nothing more to know. It was as if her reason for being suddenly evaporated into thin air. Yesterday she was seeking. Today there was nothing left to seek. Having believed, or a least hoped, Jesus was the Messiah, she now felt foolish and ashamed. Everyone told her He wasn't. How could she have been so blind and stupid - or obstinate? With all her heart, she wanted Him to be the Messiah. Well, He wasn't. Might as well face the hard facts. Jesus was an imposter, and she had been duped.

What now? Remaining in Jerusalem was out of the question. Should she go back to Samaria where she belonged? The embarrassment of facing Mishtar, Gabah and Iona was more than she wanted to endure. She could hear them saying, "See, we tried to tell you, but no, you wouldn't listen." Of course, she didn't have to go back to Sychar. Sychar wasn't the only village or city in Samaria. There was the city of Samaria.

What about Nicholas? Yes, she had Nicholas to consider too. Go to Alexandria and be with him? What would she tell him? "Jesus is dead, so I've decided to be with you?" What would he say to that? "What if Jesus hadn't been crucified; would you still be following Him?" Or, "Now that you don't have Jesus, you come to me?" She couldn't blame him if he felt like that. As a matter of fact, wasn't that the way it was? Settle her obsession for Jesus and, after that be with Nicholas - making him second choice? But he understood that and agreed to it. He promised to wait for her. What about his child? He doesn't even know I'm carrying his child. Thoroughly confused, her mind was spinning out of control.

Wandering in a semi-conscious state, consumed with grief and humiliation, Zanah saw a familiar landmark - Herod's palace. The sight of the palace upset her, but at least now she knew where she was.

She could find Simeon's pottery shop from here. Maybe Martha would help her sort things out. Simeon and Martha were the only people she knew in Jerusalem; and Martha had told her she was welcome any time. Moses was probably on his way back to Nazareth by now. When she reached the pottery shop, Simeon was busy at the wheel. He didn't see her enter.

"Simeon, Sir?"

"Oh, Zanah," he said looking up, and stopping the wheel. "We were worried about you."

"I'm sorry I worried you. May I talk to Martha?"

"Of course. Go right in."

"Thank you." Leaving the shop, she walked across the courtyard, breathing in the fragrance from the roses and anemone. How could a place be so beautiful and peaceful yet be so near to so much hate and rebellion? Would she and Nicholas have a place like this - a little garden, some flowers? Why couldn't people love one another like Jesus said? She paused before entering the court, and called out to Martha.

"Zanah, dear!" Martha exclaimed, emerging from the kitchen. "Where have you been? We were afraid something had happened to you."

Zanah told her about the mob, the trial and how she got caught up in it all. Pausing frequently to brush away the tears and clear a lump from her throat, she described the scourging, the crucifixion, the attack by Antonio and the sudden darkness. As painful as it was, she managed with difficulty to talk about it.

"I'm sorry it didn't turn out like you wanted," Martha said, hugging Zanah and rubbing her back. "Really, I am. Even though we didn't share your belief, we didn't want it to turn out like this." Releasing Zanah, she asked, "What are you going to do now?"

"I don' t know. I' m so confused."

"You know you can' t stay in Jerusalem."

"Yes, I know."

"You're a Samaritan. Why don't you go back to Samaria?"

"I thought about that, but it's a long way, and I'm afraid to go alone."

"You have reason to be afraid. A woman alone on the highway is easy prey for robbers and rapists." Casting aside the somber mood, she continued. "We might be able to find someone going that way who would let you travel with them."

"Do you really think so?" Zanah's countenance brightened.

"We can try."

Chapter Four

Martha talked to Simeon, about Zanah's plight and her desire to return to Samaria; explaining the hazards and danger of traveling alone. Did he know someone who might be going to Samaria with whom Zanah could travel? It happened a merchant on Cyprus purchased some pottery from Simeon, and a Hebrew trader was leaving in the morning to deliver the pottery. He would be passing through Samaria. Simeon felt certain the trader would permit Zanah to accompany him as far as Samaria. When he came to load the pottery, Simeon would ask him. Martha told Zanah to be ready.

When the trader arrived at the pottery shop, Simeon told him about Zanah, and he agreed to let her travel with him. Before all the pottery was loaded and secured on the donkeys, Zanah was ready to leave. She watched as the last piece of pottery was secured. Hugging Martha, and taking Simeon's hand, she thanked them for all they had done, and said goodbye.

Looking back and waving to Martha and Simeon one last time, she set out for Samaria with the trader.

The trader wasn't as talkative and congenial as Moses, or as inquisitive as Leukas, saying no more than was necessary. He was apathetic that he, a Jew, was traveling with a Samaritan - and a woman at that. Neither was he curious as to what she was doing in Jerusalem in the first place - which suited her just fine. Her sojourn in Jerusalem had been a fiasco almost from the beginning, and continued to haunt her. Even her sleep was invaded nightly by the long line of men bearing torches, a depraved look in their eyes, demanding Jesus' crucifixion - by the crack of the whip and the sight of Jesus' blood gushing forth from His wounds - by the pounding, pounding, pounding of the spikes in Jesus' hands and feet - by the sight of His body hanging on the cross, limp, lifeless - causing her to break out in a cold sweat and awake with a start. Even Antonio, with his wicked grin and lust-filled eyes, wouldn't let her rest. Would she ever be free? Would she ever find peace?

The trader may not have been curious about Zanah, but she was curious about him. Since noone had any qualms about interrogating her, she felt at liberty to interrogate him. "I know Jews hate Samaritans, and will go out of their way rather than go through Samaria. How is it you, a Jew, travel through Samaria?"

"Time is money," he said. "If you want to make money, you must take the shortest route. I want to make money."

That made sense, Zanah concurred. It was not only a typical Jewish response, but typical of most people, she reasoned. Where money was to be made, race, nationality and language differences were often overlooked - at least temporarily.

About the sixth hour of the second day, they neared Jacob's well. The trader informed Zanah he intended to stop there to rest and water the donkeys - giving her a sense of foreboding. The likelihood of meeting someone from Sychar, particularly Gabah or Mishtar - made her apprehensive. That they would mock her and cast their verbal darts at her, mortally wounding her already maimed pride, she was certain. She wasn't sure how she would react. What if she and Gabah locked horns? Another appearance before the Prefect Samuel was something she wanted to avoid. He had warned her, another summons would go hard on her. Neither did Zanah want to visit Iona and Spyros - although not for the same reason. Iona and Spyros wouldn't ridicule or deride her, she was certain; but Iona had tried to discourage her from going on such a foolish venture. If she had listened to Iona, none of this would have happened. Oh, Jesus would have been crucified, still. Antonio would still be somewhere harassing young women. But she wouldn't have been involved in any of it. She was ashamed for being so stubborn and foolish. Her pride wouldn't allow her to face Iona and admit it. Pride? Since when did she have any pride? Pride hadn't kept her from being married and divorced five times. Pride hadn't kept her from living out of wedlock with Mishtar, subjecting herself to his constant abuse. Pride hadn't kept her from accepting Iona's help after Mishtar evicted her. Pride hadn't kept her from begging Leukas to take her with him to Capernaum.

Pride hadn't kept her from sleeping with Nicholas. Pride hadn't kept her from striking out on her own, even though she might have to sleep on the ground and beg for food. Pride hadn't kept her, a Samaritan woman, from going to Jerusalem. Pride hadn't kept her from accepting Moses' help and subsequently the help of Martha and Simeon. And here she was, traveling alone with a Hebrew trader. Where is the pride in that? Too proud to face Iona and Spyros and admit she made a mistake? Well, whatever it was, she wasn't planning on seeing anyone from Sychar or Shechem if she could help it.

When they reached Jacob's well, and Zanah saw noone else was there, she breathed a sigh of relief. She needed the rest, and the cool water was refreshing; but the longer they tarried, the more uneasy she became. It seemed to her, they were there for hours, although it was only a few minutes. When the trader said they needed to move on, Zanah jumped to her feet, anxious to get underway.

They arrived in the city of Samaria the following day. The trader wished Zanah well, and she thanked him for letting her travel with him. She watched until he was out of sight. Immediately the same feeling of loneliness and abandonment she had felt when Rea left her, invaded her. It was even worse this time. She knew noone in Samaria. She had nowhere to go. Whenever she had faced a similar crisis, she reflected, someone always came to her rescue. First it was Iona, and then Rea, Moses and Martha; and just recently, the trader. Now there wasn't anyone. She didn't expect anyone. Utterly alone in a strange city, she was depressed and discouraged. As long as Jesus was alive, there was hope. Life was good and right. Now He was gone, and life was empty and hopeless. Joining Jesus in death crossed her mind. What did she have to live for? And then the baby she was carrying moved.

When Zanah learned she was pregnant, she fully intended to send Nicholas a note telling the good news. Events and circumstances intervened. She never wrote the note, pointing out she had failed to keep her promise to Nicholas. The same self-centered pride that kept her from visiting Iona was keeping her from communicating with Nicholas. She couldn't bear to tell him what a fool she had been - perhaps still was.

Meandering like a small child lost at the fair, Zanah hadn't wandered far when she saw a frail-looking man approaching. He carried a large basket on top of his head - she couldn't see what was in the basket. For no reason she could discern, he fell to the ground, dropping the basket along with its contents. Without hesitation, she rushed to his aid.

"Are you hurt?" she asked, helping him to his feet. He was so thin, she felt his bones protruding under his skin.

"I'm all right. My legs just gave out on me." He dusted himself off. Picking up the basket, Zanah saw it contained loaves of bread and flat cakes - freshly baked, from the aroma.

"This is too heavy for you. Do you have far to go?"

"No, just a furlong or two."

"Show me the way, and I'll carry the basket for you."

"You're very kind."

"I'm Zanah," she said, as they walked along.

"I'm Philippias."

"You live near here?"

"I have a small house on the edge of the city."

As they walked, Zanah learned that each day Philippias baked bread and brought it to the marketplace where he sold it to a merchant for resale to his customers. This was Philippias' livelihood, meager as it was. At his age and physical condition, he wouldn't be doing it much longer, Zanah presumed. What would he do? What would become of him, and why was she concerned about an old man she didn't even know, when she had problems of her own? What was to become of her?

Arriving at the marketplace, Philippias stopped at a booth selling fresh fruit, vegetables and spices. He told Zanah this was where he left the bread. She handed the basket to the merchant. He removed the bread, paid Philippias and returned the empty basket to Zanah. Zanah and Philippias left the market together, and headed toward Philippias' house.

"Thank you for helping me. How can I repay you?"

"You can repay me by letting me help you." The words surprised Zanah, having no premonition of making such a proposal.

"I can't do that," Philippias said.

"Why not?"

"I can' t pay you."

"I don't want any pay. I' II keep house for you, help bake the bread, and take it to the market in exchange for a place to sleep and something to eat."

"I, …I, don' t know."

"You're not able to continue by yourself."

"I know."

"I can help you, and you will be helping me."

"You think it will work?"

"We can give it a try."

Philippias' house wasn't much. Zanah saw a square, one-room limestone house with a flat roof - typical of most of the poorer houses in Samaria. Inside was a rough wooden table and a bench. A washstand with a ceramic basin and water pitcher stood against one wall. A large, stone fireplace took up another wall. The floor was dirt and, as was customary, reed mats were unrolled to sleep on. Zanah had noticed a large, stone oven outside. She was sure that was where Philippias did his baking.

The arrangement worked well. Philippias was a kind, gentle man, in his eighties, Zanah guessed. He wasn't in particularly bad health, but the years had taken their toll. At first Zanah confined her duties to keeping house and taking the bread to the market. As time went on, she learned how to mix the dough and do the baking - eventually taking over the baking too. With Zanah doing most of the work, Philippias thrived, even gaining strength. He became increasingly dependent on Zanah and admitted, without her he couldn't survive. They became close, fast friends.

Philippias never inquired about Zanah's past, allowing her to tell as much or as little about herself as she wanted. Over a period of time he learned she had lived in Sychar, but he never asked why she left there. Zanah said nothing about Jesus or having been to Jerusalem. That Zanah was pregnant was self - evident, but he assumed since she chose not to discuss it, it

173

must have been a one time affair - perhaps with a total stranger. It happens, he reasoned.

By the time the baby was due, Philippias was as anxious for Zanah as if he was the father. He made sure she got her rest, ate properly and took care of herself. He made arrangements with a neighbor woman to assist in the delivery. During Zanah's labor, he paced back and forth, wringing his hands, wiping the sweat from his brow like any expectant father.

Zanah's delivery was without complications and no more pain than is customary for that sort of thing. Zanah gave birth to a healthy, male child, whom she named Alexander, as a reminder of Alexandria where Nicholas was. She didn't let giving birth keep her down long. It was said Hebrew women had babies like a cow. Well, she was part Hebrew, so she figured she could have a baby like a cow too.

Philippias doted on the boy from the very first day. He watched after him while Zanah made the deliveries - playing with him and talking baby talk to him in a way Zanah thought was ridiculous. Philippias was good to Alexander, and Alexander was good for

Philippias. Philippias appeared to get younger, at least in spirit, with each passing day.

****

Two years passed that were the happiest and most carefree Zanah could ever remember. Mishtar, Gabah, Spyros, Iona and her life in Sychar were all behind her - never giving it any thought. It was as if it was another life, another person, another time - which in reality it was. She wasn't the same person she had been in Sychar, and she still didn't know what to attribute the change to. She stopped trying to rationalize it. It was enough that life was good. She was happy and content.

The memory of Jesus and that horrible experience in Jerusalem was almost erased from her mind - almost. The crucifixion still haunted her at times, causing her to have nightmares and cry out in her sleep - thus providing Philippias with bits and pieces to her past. In Samaria, news from Jerusalem was scant at best. People traveling from Jerusalem through Samaria brought the only news - along with the rumors. Most travelers, like the trader, were not religious, and the news and rumors related said little about Jesus and the crucifixion. Zanah learned that, following the crucifixion, persecution of Jesus' followers became extremely severe. His disciples were forced to go underground and meet in secret - many fleeing Jerusalem for their lives. Yet, for reasons Zanah failed to understand, they continued to proclaim Jesus' kingdom. Why, when they all refused to support Jesus when He was on trial? Peter even denied knowing Him. Why would they continue proclaiming His kingdom, at great risk to themselves, when He's dead? It didn't make sense. Anyway, she was through with all that.

Only on occasion, and that usually while playing with Alexander, did Zanah even think about Nicholas - for Alexander bore a remarkable resemblance to his father. His facial features and expressions were like Nicholas', and he already exhibited some of Nicholas' mannerisms. Alexander would grow tall, straight and handsome like his father. Nicholas, if he knew, would be proud of Alexander. Zanah felt guilty. He had a right to know. She wasn't being fair to him - or to

Alexander for that matter - but her false pride overruled fairness.

The bread baked and delivered, the day's work was behind them. Alexander was asleep on his mat. Zanah and Philippias went outside and sat on a bench. There was just a hint of a breeze, and the night air had not yet cooled to where it was uncomfortable for just sitting. Philippias was first to break the silence.

"You know, you have made an old man very happy," he said, laying his hand on Zanah's.

"Only because you have made me happy." She placed her hand on top of his.

"What have I done? You've done it all."

"That's not true. Where would Alexander and I be if you hadn't taken me in? What would've become of us?"

"What would've become of me? The truth is," he smiled, "We have been good for each other."

"You're right. We filled a need each of us had." Zanah wondered what Philippias was leading up to. He had never waxed this sentimental before. Oh, he frequently told her how much he appreciated all she did, and she told him how grateful she was for his loving Alexander; but something in his tone told her this conversation was different.

"You know, I don't have many years left," Philippias went on.

"Don't fool yourself. You're stronger now than when I first saw you."

"True, but I'm still old. How many years do I have left - one, two, three?"

"Let' s not think about that. Just live one day at a time."

"No, I must settle some things." He removed his hand from under Zanah's. "You know I don't have anyone - any family. As near as I know, you don't have any family either. When I die, I' d like you to have this place."

"Philippias…"

"It's not much," Philippias said, "But it will give you and Alexander a place to live and a way to earn a living."

"I, …I don't know what to say."

"Think it over. You don't need to give me your answer now."

"Oh, look, a falling star!" Zanah exclaimed. "Did you make a wish? If you make a wish before it goes out, your wish will come true."

"Do you believe that?"

"Not really, but it's been a long time since I've been able to enjoy such childish things."

****

Zanah was up at daybreak. Philippias and little Alexander were still asleep. She stoked the huge outdoor oven in preparation for the day's baking. While the oven was heating, she went inside and mixed the ingredients to make the dough. Placing the dough in the oven, she busied herself cleaning the pans and utensils. The smell of freshly baked bread soon filled the air. She removed the bread from the oven and put it in the basket. After checking to see if Philippias and Alexander were all right, she set out for the marketplace.

On the way to the market, Zanah weighed Philippias' offer. She never dreamed of owning any property - never wanted to. Most Samaritan women didn't own property. Property went to the sons, but Philippias didn't have a son. If a father had no sons, a daughter could inherit the property, but Philippias' didn't have a daughter either. In fact, she and Philippias weren't even related. Until two and a half years ago, they didn't even know each other. Zanah wondered, if legally Philippias could do what he suggested. She didn't know anything about such matters. Not many women owned a business either. How would the community regard her if she owned a business - even if it was operated from a home - and why was she concerned about that anyway? What people thought about her never concerned her before. Philippias was right. It would give her a place to live and a means for supporting herself and Alexander. It was very thoughtful of Philippias.

And then there was Nicholas. In spite of all that had happened, her guilt and shame, Zanah still believed one day she and Nicholas would be together -

at least she hoped they would. She did love Nicholas. There would never be anyone else. But after all this time apart from each other, did he feel the same about her? He had said he would wait until there was no need to wait any longer. She believed he would be true to his word, but she couldn't be sure. The possibility he might not flustered her. If she owned property and a business, how would he feel about that? Some husbands wouldn't let their wife own anything. Is that how Nicholas felt? Why was everything so complicated? Life with Mishtar may not have been pleasant, but it was simple. Zanah, still deep in thought, heard the name "Jesus" loud and clear. Startled, she saw a man with a crowd gathered around him. She recognized the man as having been with Jesus at Capernaum and in Jerusalem during Passover Week - although she couldn't recall his name, if indeed she ever knew it. He was speaking to those gathered around him about Jesus and the kingdom of heaven. How insane! Jesus is dead! Who is going to believe him now? Nevertheless, she felt herself being drawn toward him, and listening to what he was saying. He

was saying some strange things, things she had never heard before. He talked about a resurrection, a Holy Spirit and Pentecost; and it all tied in with Jesus somehow.

Zanah left the bread with the merchant and hurried back to where the man was preaching. People had started walking away, but the man was still there. She decided to question him about the message he was preaching.

"Sir, weren't you with Jesus in Galilee?"

"Yes, I am one of His disciples. My name is Philip."

"Weren't you with Him also in Jerusalem during the Passover?"

"Yes, I was also with Him then."

"Then you know He was crucified. I was in Jerusalem, and saw Him crucified. Why do you continue to talk about His kingdom?"

"You haven't heard about Jesus' resurrection?"

"Resurrection?" She was puzzled. "I know about a resurrection in the last days, but not now. Surely these aren't the last days."

"No. What you say is true, but on the third day after He was placed in the tomb, He was raised to life by the power of God."

"I don't believe it. I was foolish enough to believe once, but I'm not about to be fooled again."

"I'm telling you the truth. When the women took spices they had prepared and went to the tomb, they found the stone rolled away. Two angels told the women, "Why do you look for the living among the dead? He is not here. He is risen.""

"Maybe they were imagining things."

"No. Later Jesus appeared to all the disciples except Thomas, in the same room where He had observed the Passover with them. Still later He appeared to them again, and this time Thomas was there. I was there both times."

"I know Jesus did many amazing things, but I can't…"

"Two men walking to Emmaus saw Him and supped with Him," Philip said. "After that He was seen by upwards to four hundred people at the same time.

Later, we met Him in Galilee, and we watched as He ascended into heaven."

"I' m confused. I saw Him die. No man could live through that."

"No ordinary man, but Jesus was no ordinary man. You are like the rest of us," Philip continued. "While Jesus was with us, we didn't understand what He was telling us. He kept telling us He had to die. He said His kingdom wasn't of this world, but we didn't understand. We expected His kingdom to be like David's, here and now."

"It isn't? Now I'm more confused than ever."

"Let me explain. Jesus is God's Son. He was born of a virgin, but God was His Father. Jesus was both God and man."

"I thought Joseph was His father."

"Joseph acted as His earthly father, but God was His heavenly Father, and the heavenly Father sent His Son, Jesus, into the world to redeem mankind back to God."

"Now I'm more confused than ever." She set the basket down and wiped her forehead with her sleeve. "I don't see how Jesus could do that."

"You know God said sin must be paid for with a life?"

"Yes, I was taught that when I was a little girl."

"Do you agree, you and I are sinners?"

"I know I am. I've been told we all are."

"That's right. So, when the judgment day comes, we are going to pay for our sins with our life. Right? Unless…"

"Unless what?"

"Unless somebody loves us enough to die in our place for our sins."

"Who could possibly love me that much?"

"Jesus does. Jesus loves you so much, He gave His life as payment for your sins - and for mine, and for the whole world's."

"Are you saying what happened to Jesus was all part of a plan? Jesus knew all along He was going to die on that cross?"

"Exactly. That's what He kept trying to get us to understand. You saw Him die. He didn't have to die. He could've called on His heavenly Father, and He would've rescued Him. But He didn't call on the Father because, if He did, then you and I and everyone else would be lost from God forever. We would have to die for our sins."

"How awful. But how do you know the plan worked? I mean, suppose this was just some more of His talk?"

"That's where His resurrection comes in. Through His own resurrection, He showed the whole world He had power over sin and death."

"I still don't see how that can save me."

"It doesn't unless you believe and trust Jesus with your life."

"How can I do that? He's not even here."

"If you confess with your mouth, Jesus is Lord, and believe in your heart God raised Him from the dead, you will be saved."

"What about His kigdom?"

"We were wrong about that too. Jesus' kingdom is in our heart. He reigns in our heart, and thus rules over our life. We want to live according to Jesus' teaching and example."

"Then there really isn't any kingdom?"

"Not at this time, in this world. Now His kingdom exists only in our heart, but one day Jesus is coming back. When He does, He will judge the world. Those who belong to Him will enter into His eternal kingdom. Those who are not His will be condemned to eternal death. Then Jesus will establish His eternal kingdom here on earth. This old heaven and earth will be destroyed, and a new heaven and earth put in its place."

"I'm afraid I still don't understand. If Jesus is not here, how can I know what He teaches and wants me to do?"

"Jesus told us before he went to be with the Father, He would not leave us alone in the world. He would send His spirit to live in our heart. His spirit in our heart instructs us and teaches us everything we need to know. The Holy Spirit descended upon us believers on the day of Pentecost. So we know Jesus kept His word."

"I know I've done some terrible things, and I'm ashamed of the way I've lived. Can I be saved?"

"If you confess Jesus is Lord and believe in your heart that He lives, that God raised Him from the dead, you will be saved."

"I guess I've had Jesus in my heart ever since the day I met Him at the well. I always hoped He was the Messiah. That must've been what changed my life, and why I felt so badly when I saw the people treating Him the way they did. I still don't understand it all, but I want Jesus to save me."

Philip prayed with Zanah, and she gave her heart to Jesus. Asking Zanah to meet him at this same place in the morning, Philip said he would baptize her. Agreeing to meet him and be baptized, Zanah, her feet barely touching the ground, flew home to Philippias and Alexander. Everything - well, not everything - was clear now. There were many things about Jesus and His kingdom she didn't understand, perhaps never would. Bursting with joy and excitement, she was anxious to share the good news with Philippias.

Philippias was a Samaritan like herself, she reasoned. Samaritans believed in the coming Messiah the same as the Jews. She believed Jesus was the Messiah, why couldn't Philippias? Or would he be like Moses, or Simeon and Martha, and so many others who thought Jesus was an imposter? Well, they could think whatever they pleased. She believed, and she would gladly share her belief with Philippias.

Zanah was out of breath when she entered the house. She hugged Philippias. Scooping up Alexander, she whirled around and around with him until they were both dizzy. Philippias wondered what had come over her. Perhaps she had spent the bread money on wine. Between gasps for breath, Zanah blurted out her encounter with Philip. Philippias, unable to make sense out of what she was telling him, stopped her, told her to slow down and start over, from the beginning. She gulped and took a deep breath to calm herself. More composed and coherent, she told about her conversation with Philip, and her acceptance of Jesus as her Lord and Savior. Philippias drank in every word.

"Jesus doesn't seem like the Messiah we have been expecting," Philippias said.

"I know. That's what everyone says. But Philip said that's because we all have the wrong idea about the Messiah."

"How do you know Philip is right and all the others are wrong?"

Zanah told Philip about the part of her life pride and shame hadn't allowed her to divulge. She told him everything, from meeting Jesus at Jacob's well and the change in her life, to following Jesus and seeing Him crucified. Philippias listened without interrupting.

"Seeing the miracles Jesus performed, hearing Him teach, and listening to Philip's explanation; it all fits together. I believe with all my heart, Jesus is the Christ," Zanah said.

"And you say you' re going to be baptized in the morning?"

"Yes."

"Can an old man like me be saved?"

"I'm sure you can. Philip talked like anyone can be saved if they confess Jesus is the Christ and believe in His resurrection. Why don't you go with me in the morning?"

"Who will stay with Alexander?"

"We'll take him with us."

****

Zanah and Philippias were up early the next morning. Still feeling the excitement from the previous day, Zanah was eager to be baptized. Humming and singing, she helped prepare and bake the bread. Philippias, in a more somber mood, weighed the decision he intended to make. He wasn't as certain about Jesus as Zanah. He believed she was telling the truth - at least what she perceived to be the truth - and was speaking from her heart. Because he believed in her, and because he wanted to, he accepted her story. All his life he had looked for the Messiah, as had nearly every Jew and Samaritan. He had given up expecting to see the Messiah in his lifetime. It would be wonderful news indeed, he mused, if Jesus was the

Messiah. His was more a feeling of hope than certainty. He would wait until he talked to Philip. After delivering the bread, they found Philip at the place where he had told Zanah to meet him. Philip greeted them warmly, and Zanah introduced Philippias to him. Noticing Alexander, Philip picked up the lad and spoke with affection.

"What a beautiful child. What's his name?"

"Alexander." Zanah noticed how much Philip was like Jesus, not that he looked like Him, but in his manner and attitude. She felt as if she was talking to Jesus himself. "Philippias wants to know if he can be saved too," she added.

"Are you willing to admit you're a sinner in need of salvation, Sir?"

"Yes."

"If you confess your sins and believe in your heart Jesus is the Christ and has power over sin and death, you can be saved."

"I'm old. I don't have much time left. I'd like to know I'm right with God before I die." He paused for a moment. "Yes, I believe."

Philip led Philippias in prayer just as he did Zanah, and Philippias gave his heart to Jesus. Zanah was as thrilled for Philippias as she was for herself. The four of them walked to a pool at the edge of the city, and Philip baptized Zanah and Philippias while Alexander looked on in amusement. He wanted to play in the water too. Philip told them about a house where believers were meeting for prayer and teaching, and invited them to join the fellowship.

On the way home, both Zanah and Philippias were pensive. Zanah didn't know what was occupying Philippias' mind, but her own thoughts were on her future - specifically Philippias' offer, and her love for Nicholas. In telling Philippias about her passion for Jesus, she deliberately omitted mentioning Nicholas and him being Alexander's father. The time was right she believed, to tell him about Nicholas and her decision. Being a follower of Jesus gave her life new meaning and a new direction. It was as if she was beginning a new life.

What lay ahead for her and Alexander, or how her new life would affect her relationship with Nicholas

193

and Philippias, she had no way of knowing. Her relationship with Philippias, she believed, wouldn't change because he believed the same as she. Nicholas, on the other hand, didn't believe in Jesus. He had made it clear he not only didn't believe in Jesus, he had no desire to do so. What was it he had said? "Our gods take good enough care of us. Who needs another god?" She thought he would be understanding though. He might never accept her faith, but he wouldn't criticize or condemn her for it. Arriving home, she felt certain the decision she intended making was the right one. Zanah poured Philippias and herself a cup of wine, and they sat at the table.

"You haven't said two words since we left Philip," Zanah said. "Are you sorry for what you did?"

"You haven't been very talkative yourself. No, I was just thinking. For the first time in my life, I feel at peace with God. I'm saved. I have a family. Everything I ever wanted, and now I don't have long to enjoy it." Zanah detected the sadness in his voice. "What about you? What have you been thinking?"

"When I told you about my quest to know Jesus, I didn't mention Nicholas." She paused, looking into her cup of wine. "Nicholas is master Leukas' slave. We fell in love while we were traveling to Capernaum. He asked me to go with him and master Leukas to Alexandria, but I told him I had to learn about Jesus first." She set the cup down. "We promised to wait for each other, and we made love the night before we went our separate ways."

"So, this Nicholas is Alexander's father?"

"Yes. Nicholas doesn't know. I have never written to him or heard from him since that night - nearly three years ago."

"Why haven't you told him? Don't you think he would want to know?"

"I'm sure he would, and that's one of the decisions I've made. Now that I know the truth about Jesus, I'm not ashamed or disgraced anymore. I'm going to write telling him about his son and where we are."

"You said, one of the decisions. What other decisions have you made?"

"I've decided to stay here with you. Not because of the house or business, but because I love you, and you are so kind and loving to Alexander and me. I feel this is where I belong."

"What about Nicholas?"

"I will always love him, and I will tell him so. My love for you is different - more like a father. I never knew my father, and I guess I needed that - you know, a father's love."

"Alexander needs a father's love too."

"I know, and for now he has you. I believe this is where the Lord wants me to be - at least for the present. If Nicholas and I and Alexander are meant to be together, and I believe we are, God will make it happen in His own way, in His own time."

About the Author

Rev. C. J. Molmen attended Dallas Baptist University and also completed Bible and Theology courses through Southern Baptist Seminary Extension. He pastored Baptist churches in Texas for over 35 years, gaining the reputation as an excellent Bible scholar and teacher. He has written and delivered thousands of sermons.

Upon retirement, Rev. Molmen was led to write religious fiction based on Scripture and biblical characters. Few authors take this approach to evangelize and bring their readers into a personal relationship with God. Rev. Molmen's education and extensive background qualify him in this regard.

Printed in the United States
751300001B